If ever there was ~~a~~ ... *loving, it was Julie.*

Chris wondered what was keeping her from reaching out. What tragedy in her life had stolen her will to live, made her consciously fight against her own needs, her very nature?

One thing was certain. Kissing Julie had been like embracing life. It had filled Chris with a sense of wonder and joy. He had a feeling that healing Julie's pain would be like opening the best Christmas present he'd ever received in his entire life. But how could he help her if she fought him every step of the way? What could he do to erase the shadows in her eyes?

He stared at the twinkling Christmas tree, wondering how on earth he could find the answers she kept so close to her heart.

Dear Reader,

A gift from the heart, from us to you—this month's special collection of love stories, filled with the spirit of the holiday season. And what better place to find romance this time of year than UNDER THE MISTLETOE?

In *Daddy's Angel,* favorite author Annette Broadrick spins a tale full of charm and magic—and featuring FABULOUS FATHER Bret Bishop. Treetop angel Noelle St. Nichols visits this single dad and the children she's cherished from afar—and suddenly longs to trade her wings for love.

Annie and the Wise Men by Lindsay Longford is the heartwarming story of Annie Conroy and her kids, as their search for a temporary home on the holiday lands them face-to-face with a handsome young "Scrooge," Ben Jackson.

And Carla Cassidy will persuade you to believe once again that Santa Claus is not only alive and well—he's in love! Someone up above must have known that rugged Chris Kringle was just the man to make Julie Casswell smile again. Could it have been *The Littlest Matchmaker?*

More great books to look for this month include *A Precious Gift* by Jayne Addison, continuing the story of the lovable Falco family. Moyra Tarling shows us that *Christmas Wishes* really do come true in a moving story of a father reunited with his son by a spirited woman who believes in love. And there's love, laughter and merrymaking unlimited in Lauryn Chandler's *Romantics Anonymous*.

Wishing you a happy holiday and a wonderful New Year!

Anne Canadeo
Senior Editor

THE LITTLEST MATCHMAKER

Carla Cassidy

Silhouette

R O M A N C E™

Published by Silhouette Books

America's Publisher of Contemporary Romance

To all the little angels,
and the mothers who love them.

 SILHOUETTE BOOKS

ISBN 0-373-08978-3

THE LITTLEST MATCHMAKER

Copyright © 1993 by Carla Bracale

This edition published by arrangement with Harlequin Enterprises B.V.

® and TM are trademarks of Harlequin Enterprises B.V., used under license. Trademarks indicated with ® are registered in the United States Patent and Trademark Office, the Canadian Trade Marks Office and in other countries.

Printed in U.S.A.

Books by Carla Cassidy

Silhouette Romance

Patchwork Family #818
Whatever Alex Wants... #856
Fire and Spice #884
Homespun Hearts #905
Golden Girl #924
Something New #942
Pixie Dust #958
The Littlest Matchmaker #978

Silhouette Desire

A Fleeting Moment #784

Silhouette Intimate Moments

One of the Good Guys #531

Silhouette Shadows

Swamp Secrets #4
Heart of the Beast #11

Silhouette Books

Silhouette Shadows Short Stories 1993
"Devil and the Deep Blue Sea"

CARLA CASSIDY

is the author of ten young-adult novels. She's been a cheerleader for the Kansas City Chiefs football team and has traveled the East Coast as a singer and dancer in a band, but the greatest pleasure she's had is in creating romance and happiness for readers.

Now I lay me down to sleep,
let Mommy find a love to keep.
Since I've been gone she's been so sad.
She needs someone to make her glad.

Please let her know I'm safe right here,
and always feel her spirit near.
I want to hear her laugh once more.
She needs someone she can adore.

Santa Claus would do just fine,
he'd make her happy all the time.
He'd hold her close throughout the night.
He'd let her know that I'm all right.

I know someday she'll be with me
and we'll be as happy as can be.
But 'til that time please hear me pray.
Please bring my mommy love today.

Chapter One

"What's the matter, my child? Why are you so sad?"

The little girl turned her head at the sound of the melodious, rich voice. She released a deep sigh, one that held all the unhappiness a five-year-old could ever know.

"My momma is sad," she answered, catching her bottom lip between her teeth. "She doesn't laugh anymore, she doesn't even smile anymore, and that makes me sad." She looked up at the source of the voice. "Can't we make her happy again? Can't we do something?"

"And what do you think would make her happy?"

She frowned at this question, thinking with all her powers of concentration. Flowers? Her momma had always liked flowers, but she didn't think a bunch of them would be enough to make her momma smile again. No, it had to be something bigger, something better. Her frown deepened. Maybe the same things that made her happy would make her momma happy. A puppy? No, her momma didn't want a puppy. A red sucker with a yummy chocolate center? No, that wasn't right, either. Then what?

She smiled as a sudden thought struck her. Of course! What could possibly be better?

"Is that what you want?" the deep voice asked indulgently.

The little girl eagerly nodded, smiling brightly. Yes, it was exactly what she wanted. It was perfect. She just *knew* that Santa Claus and Christmas would make her momma happy again.

Julie Casswell didn't panic when the first fat snowflakes fell against the windshield. After all, you couldn't plan a trip into the Colorado mountains in mid-December and not expect a little snow.

It was when the snowflakes turned into shiny ice pellets that the first stir of unease whispered through her veins. The icing lasted only a few minutes, pinging and bouncing off the windshield and making a popping noise as it hit the ground, audible even with her windows tightly closed.

"Terrific," she muttered, tightening her grip on the steering wheel. Noticing that the road had taken on an ominous glaze, she slowed her speed, downshifting to low gear. Once again the ice plumped and softened, changing back to flakes the size of quarters. Although it was beautiful, she knew the white coating on top of the road glaze would be dangerous.

She frowned, glancing down at the speedometer. At this rate, it would take four hours instead of the expected two to get to her friend's cozy mountain retreat. Her frown deepened as she remembered Kathy's words of warning.

"You know the weather is unpredictable at this time of year, especially in the mountains," Kathy had admonished as she'd reluctantly handed Julie the cabin keys. "Why don't you wait and take your vacation in the spring?"

But Julie had been adamant. She'd saved up her vacation time all year to be able to take these couple of weeks off and leave Denver for the solitude of the mountain cabin. She'd worked overtime weekdays and on the weekends to give herself these two weeks. She needed to get away. By this morning, the need to escape had been overwhelming.

The feeling of suffocation had begun at Thanksgiving, with the annual ceremony of turning on the city's Christmas lights. It had continued to grow with each passing day as holly appeared wrapped around street signs, plastic animated elves had taken up residency in store windows and blinking multicolored lights painted everything in vaguely garish tones.

She gripped her hands more tightly on the wheel, squinting as she realized a thin layer of ice was forming on the windshield, clinging stubbornly and refusing to be budged by the overworked wiper blades. She eased her foot off the gas pedal as the car fishtailed slightly, crawling up the mountain pass.

Thank God I had new snow tires put on, Julie thought as the wind buffeted the car, sending cold air into every crack and crevice. The rhythmic swooshing of the wipers somehow reassured her. Thoughts of the cabin that awaited her soothed the frayed edges of her nerves. At least at Kathy's mountain hideaway there would be no festive red and green ribbons, no sparkling tinsel, no indication that the season of joy was upon the earth.

She sighed heavily. How different things had been last year at this time. Julie had welcomed the Christmas carols that greeted her each time she'd walked into the stores. The tree had been placed in the corner of the living room where it had been visible the minute anyone had walked into the room. The spirit of Christmas had not only been in the apartment, it had been in Julie's heart. But that had been before...

She shoved her thoughts aside, unable to delve any deeper into the past, afraid that grief would cause her to lose her mind. She couldn't think about Christmas. She refused to think about Christmas. She'd be perfectly satisfied if the holiday was forgotten today and every day for the rest of her life. She blinked rapidly to dispel the mist of tears that momentarily obscured her vision, then reached out and turned on the radio.

The interior of the car filled with the sound of rock and roll, and she let the familiar lyrics fill her head, keeping any other thoughts at bay.

At least inside the cabin she would find the solitude she sought. Once she closed the door behind her, she wouldn't have to look at another reminder of Christmas. By the time she left the cabin and returned to Denver after the first of the year, the decorations would be repacked and Christmas would be boxed away for another year. This thought brought comfort, and she stepped on the gas, anxious to get to her holiday hideaway.

Within another half an hour, she began to look around for someplace to sit out the storm. An abandoned cabin, an old garage or shed . . . anyplace she could pull in and wait for the snow to stop falling. It was serious now, obscuring visibility as huge gusts of wind rocked the tiny car. It was growing more and more difficult for Julie to discern where the road was, as all of the landscape was blanketed with a fresh layer of white icing.

Actually one of the reasons she had wanted to come to the cabin was because it was off the beaten path; she knew there would be no welcoming motel signs flashing vacancies anywhere in the area.

I'll just continue to drive slowly, she told herself. *At least the car is still moving forward.* As she crested the top of a steep hill and saw that the road on the other side was a straight, downward plunge, she once again gripped the steering wheel tightly, pumping her brakes so she wouldn't descend too quickly. On one side of the road was a sheer cliff, with only a narrow guardrail standing sentry to prevent a deadly acci-dent. The other side of the road was flatter, but studded with majestic evergreens, leaving little room for a car to weave its way in between.

At first, as the car began its downward path, Julie felt completely in control. "Come on, you can do it," she muttered to herself. She crept along, her foot barely tapping the brakes to keep her speed under control. She was halfway down the mountainside when she realized the car was picking up speed...too much speed. She pumped hard on the brakes, feeling the ominous sliding of the rear end, but not slowing the vehicle at all.

It's out of control, she thought. She felt no real fear—in fact she felt nothing except a vague disinterest. She knew a hard brake would send her into a deadly spin, and the road was too narrow to accommodate such a spin. She knew if the car did begin to twist and turn, she would eventually end up at the bottom of the cliff. She realized she had only one choice: to try to steer the car onto the flatter land on the right side of the road and hope that she could control it enough to weave around the large pine trees.

As the bottom of the hill approached, she once again looked down at her speedometer. Too fast... much too fast. For the first time in a year, she felt the stir of an emotion. She caught her bottom lip between her teeth, her grip on the steering wheel so tight, her knuckles were white with the strain. She'd never be able to make the curve at the bottom of the hill. She had to stop her downward slide and she knew there was only one way to do that.

Decision made, she watched for a place where the trees were less dense. Seeing what she thought looked like the best place, she spun the wheel, cutting the tires in a hard right turn. For a moment the car hesitated, as if reluctant to do as she wanted. It slid another ten feet or so forward, then followed the direction of the wheels.

She never saw the tree. There was a loud noise, a screeching rent of metal on metal. An excruciating pain exploded in her head . . . then blackness.

The little girl frowned. "Uh-oh," she uttered softly, then looked up with doubtful eyes. This wasn't what she'd wanted for her momma. This wasn't what she'd had in mind at all. "Are you sure you know what you're doin'?"

The deep voice laughed gently. "Don't be afraid. Just watch, my little one. Trust me and watch."

Chris crested the huge hill, slowing the horses and pulling his heavy coat more tightly around his neck. When he'd left to take the sleigh out to test the new runners, he hadn't anticipated the storm moving in quite so quickly. He wished he'd remembered a woolen scarf. He would welcome its thick warmth wrapped around his neck right now.

The sleigh bells rang with melodic tones, breaking the hushed silence that had come with the snow. The horses snorted, their breaths freezing and rising in clouds of vapor.

Despite the fact that his mustache and beard were crusted with snow and ice, in spite of the fact that his cheeks were raw, whipped red by the frigid winds, Chris felt invigorated by the storm, knowing it would transform everything to a wintry picture postcard. It would be terrific for business.

Although Mabel would complain about the melting snow and mud on all the floors, the kids would be happy with the winter wonderland appearance. After all, what was the North Pole without snow?

Coming over the top of the large hill, he noted how the limbs of the surrounding evergreen trees were laden with white frosting. The colorless layers played tricks with depth perception as all the landscape seemed to blend together.

He frowned suddenly as he saw a splash of metallic red peeking out among the trees near the bottom of the hill. What the heck . . . ? He squinted, his visibility hindered by the still-falling snow.

He approached, realizing the red was the back end of a car. His heart began pumping wildly in his chest as he saw that the front of the car was smashed, the hood buckled upward from where it had made vicious contact with the towering evergreen.

"Whoa," he said, pulling on the reins and braking the sleigh. He jumped down, his boots sinking into the thick blanket of snow that had fallen so quickly.

As he moved closer to the vehicle, his heart skipped a beat. There was a figure slumped over the steering wheel. Chris heard the hiss of hot steam escaping from the cracked radiator. The accident apparently had happened only moments before. He wondered vaguely why he hadn't heard anything. He must have been on the other side of the hill when the car had hit the tree. His heart pounded erratically as he realized that whoever was inside the wreckage might be fatally injured.

He opened the driver door, metal screeching against metal. For a moment he wasn't sure what to do. It was obvious the driver was a woman. She was slumped forward and blond hair spilled over the collar of the dark blue coat she wore. It was equally obvious that she was hurt. She didn't stir at all.

He stood beside the car, indecisive. Never remove an accident victim.... Wasn't that what he'd always heard? There could be internal injuries, spinal injuries ... he could do more harm than good. But if he didn't get her out of the car, she wouldn't get help. Chris doubted that anyone else would be traveling these roads until the snow stopped falling.

In this cold, it wouldn't take her long to die from exposure if he didn't get her to someplace warm. If she wasn't already... He let the half-completed thought drift away.

Decision made, he pulled off one of his gloves and gently lifted her hand. Feeling the inside of her wrist, he expelled a sigh of relief as he found a strong pulse. At least she was alive.

With gentle hands he eased her head back, his breath catching as he saw the poinsettia-red bruise already blossoming on her forehead. He looked at the windshield and spied the point of contact, a starburst of cracked glass where her head had hit.

The second thing he noticed was her beauty. Although her features were slack in unconsciousness, it was easy to see their attractiveness. Pale blond eyebrows arched over eyes decorated with long, spiky lashes...eyes that didn't open even as he tentatively felt down each of her jean-clad legs, wanting to make certain they weren't twisted or broken. Assuring himself that her legs weren't trapped, he eased one arm around her back, grateful that she was a slight little thing who would be easy to carry.

She moaned as he lifted her out of the wreck and into his arms, but her eyes didn't flutter, nor did she give any sign of regaining consciousness. As he removed her, he saw her purse, dark blue against the tan interior of the car. Realizing he might need some ID, he grabbed it, too. Then he quickly hurried back to the sleigh with her.

The horses neighed and stamped their feet impatiently as he covered her with the thick blanket Mabel always insisted he carry with him when he went out in the sleigh. For once, he was grateful for the old woman's prudence.

"Patience, boys," he said absently to the animals as he made sure the blanket was tucked carefully around his passenger. Again he was struck by the beauty of her delicate features. She looked like an angel, so fair and beautiful. But she was a broken angel, and she was pale... far too pale.

He needed to get her someplace warm immediately. He looked up at the gray sky, realizing the snow could continue for hours.

With a sense of urgency, he jumped back up on the sleigh and urged the horses forward.

If there had been a hospital nearby, he would have made tracks to get her there. But the nearest hospital was a good thirty miles away. There was really only one place he could take her: home... home to the North Pole.

Bells. It was Julie's first conscious thought. She frowned, longing for the total darkness that had been so soothing, where any and all thought had been impossible. But the darkness was ebbing and refused to be recaptured. Bells. Where were they coming from? What did they mean?

She reached beyond the blackness of her mind, trying to discern where she was, what was happening.

The car... She had been in the car careening wildly down a snow-slickened hill. Maybe the sound was that of the snow tires singing through the snow. No...that was impossible. She wasn't driving. Confusion battled with the receding darkness. Had she wrecked the car? Was she dead?

Her eyes flew open to a world of white, a cold, unrecognizable world. She couldn't be dead. She was far too cold...and her face was wet from snow falling from the sky. She started to sit up, then moaned as nauseating, overwhelming pain shot through her head.

"It's all right. Don't move." A deep voice spoke to her, causing her panic to intensify. She struggled upward, the pain in her head causing her stomach to heave. Looking around, she realized she was in the back of a sleigh.

"What...what happened? Where am I?" The words escaped her on a sigh.

"You've been in a car accident. It's going to be okay. I'm going to help you."

She turned her head, looking at the broad back of the driver, her mind struggling to comprehend what he was saying. An accident? Yes...yes, of course, she must have hit her head. She didn't know how she had gotten into the back of the sleigh. She had no idea who the driver was... but she was alive. There was no sudden burst of joy at this thought, only a weary resignation.

She reached a hand up and carefully touched her forehead, wincing as her fingers encountered the tender area.

"Please, just lie still. We'll have you inside, warm and safe in just a few minutes, but you really shouldn't move around." The driver of the sleigh turned around and smiled at her.

Julie felt her world tilt as she stared at him. Bright blue eyes sparkled at her from beneath thick, white eyebrows. A full white beard and mustache decorated the lower portion of his face. The eyes were kind, the smile warm and reassuring, but Julie stared at him as if he were a nightmare image. She slid back down to a prone position, her breath escaping her lungs on a wheeze. Maybe she was dead after all. She was dead and this was her own personal hell.

Or it's a nightmare, she thought in horror. Either that or she had hit her head so hard, she was now hallucinating. She suddenly recognized that the sound she'd been hearing was the sleigh bells ringing above the moan of the wind. Now they were discordant in her aching head.

She closed her eyes and choked back a hysterical burst of laughter, knowing if she allowed its release, tears would surely follow. It was crazy; it was all insane.

She'd been running away from Denver, trying to escape the merriment of the holidays, the reminder of Christmas. Yes, she'd been running away from Christmas—only to wreck her car and be rescued by Santa Claus.

Chapter Two

Julie opened her eyes and immediately winced as brilliant morning light caused an explosion of pain in the center of her forehead. She squeezed them closed again, her hand reaching up to catch her head before it rolled off her shoulders.

A slight concussion...that was what the funny white-haired man had guessed the night before. It didn't feel like anything as ordinary as a concussion. It was more like how she imagined a lobotomy might feel.

She frowned as she tried to remember other things from the night before. She'd been pretty out of it and only had vague images. There had been an old woman with white hair and kind, blue eyes. She'd smelled of lilacs and had clucked sympathetically over Julie, helping her out of her clothes and into a huge nightgown that had smelled of lemony freshness. Julie had hurt too much to protest or question much of anything. She'd been dizzy and nauseous and all she'd wanted to do was sleep. There had been another man, too—the one who'd carried her in his sleigh. She frowned, pain shooting through her head.

Opening her eyes once again, she looked around the room where she had slept. It was a pleasant bedroom, decorated in mauves and green tones. Obviously, she wasn't in the hospital. It was a neat room, decorated in neither an overtly masculine or feminine way. Where exactly was she? She remembered very little of her surroundings when she'd been brought in the night before. All she remembered was the pain and the fact that she had been horrendously cold.

She knew that eventually she would want some answers, but at the moment her head ached too much for her to care. She was safe, she was warm, and that was all that was important.

She gazed toward the window, realizing that the light shining in was not sunshine, but rather the peculiar illumination that always radiated from snowfall. It was still coming down. She could see the flakes as they danced downward to the ground, adding to the layered white that shrouded the entire outside world.

She frowned as she spied something else... something standing near a distant grove of evergreen trees. She struggled to a sitting position, trying to ignore the thunder in her head as she leaned toward the window, intent on identifying the creature. A moose? she wondered as she saw the majestic rack of antlers. No, it wasn't quite big enough to be a moose. It looked more like... like a reindeer.

She closed her eyes once again and sank back down on the bed, her mind suddenly filled with the memory of the man who had rescued her the evening before. Santa Claus... a sleigh... Rudolph... She reached up and touched her forehead once again, wondering if it was possible that she had permanently scrambled her brains. Where was she? What kind of place was this?

Julie turned as the bedroom door opened and the old, curly-haired woman she remembered from before bustled in. "Ah, good, you're awake," the woman said, her smile deepening the wrinkles in her face. She clucked sympathetically. "And you've got quite a goose egg on your forehead. We didn't formally introduce ourselves last night. Poor thing, you were pretty banged up. I'm Mabel Trimble, and you're...?"

"Julie...Julie Casswell." Julie struggled to a sitting position on the bed. "Where...where am I?" she asked as Mabel reached behind her and gently plumped the pillows.

"Oh, honey, it's a good thing Chris happened by your car yesterday, or you'd have froze to death. This is his place, the North Pole."

Julie's head began spinning once again. "The North Pole? Aren't we in Colorado anymore?"

Mabel's laughter resembled the tinkling sound of tiny bells. "Oh, my, now I've gone and confused you. Not the real North Pole," she explained. "That's just what we call it, but you're still in Colorado. In fact, we're just a few miles from where you wrecked your car."

"My car!" Julie suddenly remembered what circumstances had brought her here. She started to swing her legs out from under the covers, but stopped, moaning as every muscle in her body screamed in protest.

"There, there now," Mabel exclaimed, tucking Julie back in and drawing the covers up around her neck. "You aren't ready to get out of bed. Doc Rogers said you need to stay down for a day or two, to let your head heal and your body recover. You took quite a jolt when you hit that tree.''

"But I can't stay here," Julie protested weakly. She didn't know these people, she didn't know exactly where she was... She wanted to run, to escape, to seek the isolation and solitude of Kathy's cabin.

"Of course you'll stay here," Mabel said, a calm finality in her voice. "There's nothing you can do for the next day or two anyway. The storm is still blowing. You're safe here."

Wearily, Julie nodded, too sore to argue, her head pounding too loud for her to even try to think. She'd think later, when she felt better.

Perhaps if she just took a little nap... Then she could figure out what she was going to do. One thing was certain—she wasn't staying here. She couldn't. Especially not at a place called the North Pole. With a small sigh, she once again closed her eyes.

When she awoke again, the room was filled with the ethereal light of a false dusk. The snow still fell outside the window, the sky a dismal gray emptying to the earth its frozen tears.

She lay for a moment without moving. When finally she did slowly move her head, she was grateful that the intense pain was gone, leaving behind only a lingering dull ache.

She raised her head slightly and looked around, gasping in surprise as she saw the man sitting in the rocking chair in the corner of the room. She lay her head back down and quickly feigned sleep once again, her mind whirling in confusion. Who was he? He certainly wasn't the little white-haired man who'd gently examined her head when she'd been brought here.

She lifted one eyelid and peeked at him once again, her mind suddenly filled with images of her rescuer the night before. The face was the same...but where was the white beard? His dark beard and equally dark hair confused her. Had she only dreamed of Santa Claus bringing her here in his sleigh?

He suddenly looked at her, a smile curving his lips, and in his smile she saw that he was the man who'd rescued her the night before. There couldn't be another with such bright blue eyes, a smile that radiated warmth. It must have been the snow, she realized suddenly. When she'd seen him the night before in the storm, his beard and hair had been dusted with snow.

"Hello," he said softly.

"Hello," she returned.

"How are you feeling?"

"Better, I think," she answered thoughtfully. "At least the pounding in my head has lessened and I'm not quite so dizzy."

He nodded, apparently satisfied. "Do you think you feel like getting up and coming down to the kitchen for something to eat, or would you rather have Mabel bring you up a tray?"

"Oh, I don't need anything. I don't want to be a bother," she quickly protested. She wanted to get up and get out of here. She wanted nothing to do with these people. She only wanted to be left alone.

"It's no bother. You've been asleep all day. Your body needs food to heal."

She considered this, then slowly nodded. "Okay, I'll eat, but I don't want to be a bother. I'll come to the kitchen."

Again he nodded, then stood up, motioning to a doorway. "The bathroom is just in here if you want to clean up. Dinner will be ready in about fifteen minutes." With another of his warm smiles, he left the room.

Julie hesitated only a moment, then eased herself to a sitting position, pleased that her headache really did seem better.

As she swung her legs over the side of the bed and stood up, she thought of the man who had just left the room. He'd definitely been the one in the sleigh, the man she'd mistaken for Santa Claus. With his snow-topped beard and in her disorientation, she'd mistaken him for old St. Nick himself.

But there was nothing old about him. With his brilliant blue eyes and rich dark hair he looked no older than his mid-thirties. And those broad shoulders beneath the red plaid shirt and slim hips clad in the tight, worn jeans gave him a build that was definitely un-Santa-like.

Dismissing thoughts of the attractive man, she staggered to the bathroom, her muscles screaming their displeasure at the physical activity. She reached the sink with its wall mirror and peered at her reflection. A lump the size of her fist decorated the center of her forehead. Radiating out from the lump was a livid red bruise. "Terrific," she groaned.

She washed her face, carefully scrubbing around the tender area, then went back into the bedroom and looked around for her clothes. They were nowhere to be found. The gown she wore was hardly proper attire. Although clean and comfortable, it hung on her petite frame, the armholes large enough to make the gown almost obscene. It floated around her body like a tent and Julie suspected it belonged to the plump Mabel.

She couldn't eat dinner dressed this way. She sat down on the edge of the bed, unsure what else to do.

She looked up as a rapid knock sounded on her door and Mabel bustled in. In her arms were Julie's clothes. "Chris told me he invited you downstairs for dinner, but of course he didn't think about clothes. Just like a man." She handed Julie the sweater and jeans. "I just pulled them out of the dryer, so they're all nice and warm."

"You didn't have to do that," Julie protested, taking the clothes from the old woman.

"Nonsense, that's what I'm here for. To cook and clean and keep Chris in line." She beamed a smile at Julie. "After you get dressed, come on downstairs and dinner will be ready. Just go down the big staircase and turn left at the bottom. You'll find the kitchen right there."

Julie dressed slowly, finding each movement still incredibly painful. She must have really taken a jolt. She groaned as she tried to visualize her car. She only hoped the damage could be fixed quickly so she could get on her way. Although both Mabel and Chris seemed nice enough, she only wanted—no, she *needed* to be alone.

Finally dressed, she eased the bedroom door open and stepped out into a long hallway. She had no idea what this place was, but whatever it was, it was huge.

She followed the hallway to a large landing and as she looked out over the railing to the rooms below, she felt the blood drain from her face. She gripped the railing, feeling the carved wooden banister beneath each fingertip as she fought against the despair that winged through her.

Christmas... It was everywhere she looked in the room below. A huge tree took center stage, majestically reaching toward the high ceilings with perfectly formed branches. Around the base of the tree was the beginning of a miniature train track.

In the far corner of the room was obviously Santa's workshop area, complete with pint-size animated elves all moving to perform various tasks of toy making.

One wall of the room held an enormous stone fireplace, a dozen red stockings hanging in a row from the thick, wooden mantel. She could see the glittering names on the stockings from where she stood. Dasher, Dancer, Prancer...

Julie sank down to sit on the top stair, a horrible suffocating sensation sweeping over her. The elves' brightly painted faces seemed to mock her. The glistening glitter of the stockings sent a shaft of pain through her soul. The smell of the tree drifted up to her, the fresh cedar mingling with the scents of cinnamon and spices that lingered in the air. She was vaguely aware of an instrumental rendition of "Joy to the World" coming from speakers that rested on the floor next to the fireplace. She pressed the palms of her hands tightly against her ears, needing to insulate herself from the joyous sounds. How could there be any joy in her world? Tears blurred her vision and she squeezed her eyes tightly closed, a single name echoing over and over again in the empty chambers of her heart.

"Ah, there you are. We were wondering if you were coming down."

She looked up to see the attractive man from her room standing at the foot of the stairs, his brow wrinkled in concern. "Are you all right?" he asked, taking the stairs two at a time until he stood right next to her. "Do you need some help?"

"I . . . I . . ." She looked up at him helplessly, unsure what to say. She couldn't explain the grief that tore at her insides like an insidious, unrelenting monster. She couldn't tell him that the sights, the sounds of Christmas only served to remind her of— She reached a hand up to her head, where the dull pounding had intensified.

"We obviously overestimated your strength," he said gently. In one smooth movement, he picked her up in his arms and carried her back toward the bedroom.

His arms were strong and sure and his shirt smelled of spicy cologne and woodsmoke. His eyes were such a warm blue that for a moment Julie wanted to fall into them, dwell in the tranquil sea of their color. She didn't want to have to think, she didn't want to have to feel.

As he placed her back on the bed, he frowned worriedly and pulled the blankets up around her. "As soon as the snow stops falling and the roads are accessible, perhaps I should get the doctor up here to take a look at your forehead."

Julie stared at him dully. "Wasn't that a doctor who looked at me last night?" He'd certainly acted like one, feeling her pulse, taking her temperature, using a pen light to look at the pupils of her eyes.

He grinned, running a hand down his neatly trimmed beard. "Actually Doc Rogers is a doctor, but his usual patients either neigh or bark."

"Neigh or bark...?" Julie stared at him. "You mean he's a vet?"

He nodded. "But if it's any consolation, he's the best veterinarian in the entire state of Colorado."

Julie reached up and touched her forehead, somehow not assured by his words. Still, she was fairly certain that she suffered nothing worse than a concussion. Everything else seemed to be working all right, and other than her headache, she wasn't suffering any dire symptoms. "I'm sure I don't need to see a doctor," she finally said. "I just got a little dizzy there for a minute," she improvised.

He studied her for a long moment and again Julie felt the warmth that seemed to radiate from his eyes. "I'll have Mabel bring you up a tray."

"I'm really not very hungry," she replied. Although she was rather hungry, she didn't want to bother these people whom she had no desire to connect with. She didn't want to be with anyone. She wanted only the cocoon of her self-imposed isolation.

She looked back at the window, sighing heavily as she saw the snow still falling. "Perhaps by morning the roads will be cleared and I'll be on my way."

"Don't be in a big hurry, Julie. We have plenty of room here and you aren't going to inconvenience anyone. Give yourself a chance to completely heal."

She gazed back at him, surprised by his use of her name. "How . . . how do you know my name?"

He shrugged and looked apologetic. "When I brought you in last night, I looked in your purse for some ID. I hope you don't mind." She shook her head and he continued, "I couldn't find an emergency contact. Is there anyone I should call? Anyone who might be expecting you?"

"No, nobody. I was on my way to spend the holidays alone at a friend's cabin." Julie felt a hot blush steal over her face. This whole situation seemed so strange. She was in bed in an unusual place, talking to a man she'd initially mistaken for Santa Claus. "Uh...I'm afraid we haven't been formally introduced."

"My name is Chris...Chris Kringle." He smiled again and moved toward the door. "Don't worry about anything, Julie. We'll talk later when you're feeling better." With that, he left the room.

Julie stared after him. Chris Kringle? Was that his idea of a joke? Maybe she hadn't heard him correctly. Maybe Doc Rogers had made a mistake and she really was suffering from permanent brain damage.

In any case, no matter what the truth was, it was more important than ever that she get out of here as soon as possible.

Chris walked down the stairs and back into the kitchen.

"Is she coming?" Mabel asked as he eased himself into a chair at the large wooden table.

He shook his head. "No, I don't think she's quite up to it yet. She started down, but got pretty wobbly on the stairs. Would you mind taking a tray to her?" Mabel shook her head, her tongue clucking as she pulled a serving tray out from the cabinet and began filling a plate.

"Poor little thing. She's far too thin and all eyes. From the looks of that bruise on her forehead, she's going to have a headache for a month to come. Of course, that's none of our concern. If it stops snowing tonight they'll have the roads cleared off by noon or so and she'll be on her way."

"Hmm," Chris murmured absently, his thoughts on her lovely wide eyes. With her pale blond hair, he'd somehow expected them to be blue. He hadn't been able to tell what color they were the night before when he'd brought her home through the storm. When he'd finally seen them a little while ago, he'd been pleasantly surprised by their rich, deep brown color.

"I'm sure she's got family somewhere waiting for her arrival," Mabel added, scooping up a healthy portion of mashed potatoes onto the plate for their guest.

"No, I asked her. She said there was nobody I should contact." He paused a moment thoughtfully. "Nobody should have to spend the holidays alone."

Mabel stopped her dinner preparations and turned to look at him. "Christopher Kringle, you get that look off your face this instant," she demanded. "You know what I'm talking about," she continued at his perplexed look. "It's the same expression you get every time you see an injured animal along the side of the road ... the same one you get when you hear of a kid at the school not going home for the holidays. That woman has got a head wound, but by morning she should be well enough to get back on her way. You did a good deed by getting her out of the storm. But that's where your responsibility begins and ends.''

Chris nodded, but he wondered. As Mabel turned back to her task, grumbling about his penchant for healing wounded sparrows, he ignored her and instead focused his thoughts again on the woman upstairs.

When he'd seen her sitting at the top of the stairs, he'd sensed that the pain he saw radiating from her eyes had nothing to do with her head injury. He'd wanted to take her in his arms and kiss away the mist of tears that blurred her beautiful eyes.

It had been raw heartache he'd seen darkening the brown of her eyes, and he now wondered if a divine hand had somehow sent her to him to heal.

Chapter Three

Julie held Livvy in her arms, the little girl's baby-fine hair tickling Julie's nose with its sweet scent. There was nothing better than holding Livvy while she slept, when the abundant energy that marked the child's personality was momentarily silenced in slumber.

She loved the way Livvy's long lashes cast dark shadows on her cherub cheeks, the way her breath puffed out of her lips in little whiffs of sweetness. She adored the row of coppery freckles that decorated the tip of Livvy's upturned nose...each and every characteristic that made Livvy...Livvy.

With the tip of her finger, Julie traced the side of Livvy's face, watching the smile that moved her little mouth upward even in sleep. Julie's heart swelled with maternal love, swelled to the point where there was no room for anything else inside her. She'd never known a love like this, one so fulfilling, one so all-encompassing.

As she stared down at Livvy, the child's face slowly began to take on a ghostly white color, the weight of her in Julie's arms lightened, growing insubstantial.

"No," Julie whispered, gripping the child more tightly in her arms, trying to hang on, but it was like trying to hold on to an elusive puff of smoke.

Julie fought to retain the image, wanting to savor the feel of her child's warm body, the scent of her skin, the very essence of her soul, but it disappeared and Julie cried out.

"No...please..." The plea came from her soul, ripping up her heart. She came fully awake, empty-armed, her grief overpowering any lingering effect of her dream. She drew the pillow against her stomach, curling into a fetal ball, needing something, anything, to ease the pain she knew no medicine could ease.

She hadn't had the dream in months, had almost believed it was gone forever. Apparently the holidays had reopened the wound, renewed the pain.

When the last bittersweet remnant of the dream had left her, she rolled over and looked at the window, grateful that there was no snow flying by the glass. It looked as though the sun was trying to peek through the dreary gray clouds. Good—if luck was on her side perhaps she could leave here by noon today. She needed to get out of here as soon as possible.

With this thought in mind, she got out of bed, pleased to discover her headache seemed to be almost gone. Moments later, dressed and looking in the bathroom mirror, she noticed that the bruise on her forehead was turning a ghastly shade of purple. At least that was a sign of healing. Hopefully it would be completely gone by the time she returned to her bookkeeping job after the first of the year.

As she left the bedroom, following the scent of fresh-brewed coffee down the stairs, she was grateful to see that the sun was making steady progress across the sky. She felt her first burst of optimism, an optimism that carried her quickly through the Christmas-laden great room and into a large, cheerful kitchen.

"Hello?" she called tentatively, seeing nobody around. Spying the automatic coffeemaker and a nearby mug tree, she helped herself to the fresh brew.

She took the coffee over to the table and sat down, looking around the kitchen with interest. It was a large, cheerful room, obviously able to accommodate cooking for a large crowd of people. Again she found herself wondering exactly what this place was. It seemed far too big to be somebody's home, yet there was a homey feel to it.

She turned as the back door opened and Chris entered, stamping the snow off his boots and bringing a burst of arctic air in with him. "Ah, you must be feeling better," he said, removing his gloves and shrugging off his jacket. "I see you found the coffee."

"Yes, thank you, and I'm feeling much better this morning." She watched as he bent down to untie the laces of the fur-lined boots, noticing how he seemed to fill the room with his masculinity. He looked far more like a macho, ax-wielding lumberjack this morning than a benign, twinkling eyed Santa. His hair was wind-whipped, dark as soot, and for a moment Julie wondered if it would be soft beneath her fingertips. She quickly sipped her coffee, uncomfortable with the sudden, intimate vision of her hand stroking the rich darkness of his hair.

He quickly kicked off the boots, then set them side by side by the back door, where already a puddle of water was gathering on the linoleum beneath them as their snowy cover melted off.

"I don't know about you, but I'm starving," he said, going to the oven and opening the door. "Mmm, I knew I smelled some of Mabel's cinnamon rolls." He took out a pan of warm, icing topped rolls and set it on the table. Then he poured himself a cup of coffee and sat down across from Julie.

"Help yourself," he told her, smiling not only with his mouth, but with his eyes, as well. He had the nicest eyes Julie had ever seen. Bright blue and expressive, they made a strange warmth surround Julie—a warmth she found distinctly uncomfortable.

She took one of the rolls from the pan. She hadn't realized just how ravenous she was until he'd set them before her on the table. Their fragrance filled the air, making her mouth water in anticipation. She bit into it, an unconscious moan of pleasure escaping her as she tasted the iced cinnamon sweetness.

"Great, huh?" He grinned. "It's one of the reasons I don't fire Mabel for her impertinence."

Julie raised an eyebrow at him dubiously. From what she'd seen of the old woman, she had a feeling Chris had very little control over her. "I see it's stopped snowing," she observed as she reached for a second roll. "I should be able to leave this afternoon."

"I doubt it," he countered. "There's a foot of new snow out there. There's no way they'll have these roads cleared off today. Perhaps tomorrow or the next day. Besides, I'm afraid you're going to have more of a problem than snow-covered roads."

"What?"

"When I drove up to your car, your radiator was spewing water from a rupture and your hood was buckled to stand almost straight up in the air. Your car isn't going to be drivable without some major repair work."

Disappointment swelled inside Julie. Disappointment and a horrible feeling of being trapped. "Then perhaps you could take me to a motel. I've imposed on your kindness long enough."

"That's nonsense. We've got plenty of room here. It would be ridiculous for you to go to a motel. I'll call Charley down at the garage this afternoon and make arrangements for him to take your car in and get busy on fixing it."

"But...I..." Julie groped for words, not wanting to offend him, but not wanting to accept his hospitality, either. There was something about this place, this man, that threatened her.

"It's all settled. You'll be our guest until your car is repaired." He said it with a note of finality that made it impossible for Julie to protest any further.

"If it warms up this afternoon, I'll get the sleigh out and collect your things from your car."

"I'd like to go with you," she said, wanting to check the condition of the vehicle herself.

He frowned in concern. "I'm not sure that's such a great idea." He looked at the bruise on her forehead.

She reached up and rubbed it self-consciously. "I know this looks horrible, but it doesn't hurt so much anymore. Really, I feel just fine, and I think the fresh air would be good for me."

He nodded and got up to pour himself some more coffee. Julie noticed the breadth of his shoulders beneath the plaid flannel shirt, the way his worn jeans hugged his slender hips, how his dark hair curled slightly at the nape of his neck. Why couldn't she have been snowed in with a gnome? Or a monk? Why did it have to be this attractive, sexy man? She stared into her cup. She didn't need complications in her life. She didn't need anything except to be left alone.

"So, where are you from?" he asked, rejoining her at the table.

"Denver. I work there in a bookkeeping firm. I was on my way to a co-worker's cabin for the holidays when I met that tree."

"You were going to spend the holidays alone?" His dark eyebrows raised quizzically.

She nodded, her gaze not meeting his.

"Ah, there you both are. I was wondering where everyone had gone." Mabel burst into the kitchen, a whirlwind of chatter that alleviated Julie's discomfort at Chris's probing eyes. "I went up to see if Julie was feeling better, but she wasn't there." She stopped suddenly, her hands on her ample hips, looking at the mess Chris's boots had made on her floor. "Christopher Kringle, how many times do I have to tell you to keep those boots outside and not on my nice, clean floor?"

Grabbing a handful of paper towels, Mabel set the boots outside the back door and swiped up the water. Chris grinned at Julie. "See what I mean about impertinence?"

"I'll give you impertinence," Mabel retorted, tossing the soiled towels in the trash and banging down the trash-can lid. As she walked behind Chris, she cuffed him lightly on the back of the head, but Julie noticed that the old woman's eyes twinkled with obvious fondness.

"You better be careful, Mabel. Impertinence is cause for immediate dismissal," Chris said teasingly.

"Hrumph. Who else would you find to put up with your nonsense?" She winked broadly at Julie. "And who else would get up at the crack of dawn to fix you those cinnamon rolls you love more than life itself?"

Chris laughed and once again looked at Julie. "See, she's got me." He turned back and grinned at the old woman.

Julie was surprised to feel a smile curve her lips. It felt alien and made her realize how very long it had been since she'd felt like smiling. Guilt followed, making the reflex disappear immediately.

She suddenly needed to escape the frivolity of the conversation, wanted to run from the obvious affection and warmth that existed between Mabel and Chris, a warmth she felt they were trying to include her in.

Scooting back her chair, she stood up. "If you'll both excuse me, I think I'll just go back upstairs." She escaped before either of them could say anything, running from the kitchen and into the great room. There, the Christmas decor mocked her with its cheerfulness, taunted her with its merry colors and images.

She raced up the stairs, seeking the solace of the bedroom where there were no reminders of the holiday season to drive her insane, no kindness of strangers to tug at her buried emotions.

She stood at the window and stared out at the sparkling drifts of snow. It was beautiful, but it held her prisoner. How long before the roads became passable? How long before her car could be repaired and she could be on her way? As she remembered the warmth of Chris's smile, the concern that lit his gorgeous blue eyes, she realized no matter how long it took... it would be far too long.

"It's all been set in motion," the deep voice said. "And now it's time to go."

The little girl stood up in dismay. "Oh, please, just a little bit longer... just a smidgen longer." She held up her fingers to indicate a smidgen. "I just want to see her smile real big. I want to hear her laugh—then I'll know she'll be okay." She smiled appealingly, the one that had always managed to get her an extra cookie from her momma.

The deep voice laughed indulgently. "All right," he agreed. "A smidgen longer." The laughter was like a soft, gentle wind that wrapped her up in loving arms and she smiled happily as she sat back down.

"Come in," Julie called as a knock fell on her bedroom door.

Chris poked his head in. "You still think you're up to a sleigh ride?"

Julie sat up on the bed and nodded eagerly. "Sure."

"It's warmed up some outside, so if we bundle up real good, we should be able to collect your things from the car."

"Great." She followed him down the stairs and into the kitchen, where Mabel awaited them, her arms filled with heavy woolen scarves, thick gloves and extra socks. "A couple of fools, that's what you are," she said as she handed Julie her coat. "Her, I understand," she said, speaking to Chris, but motioning to Julie. "She took a bad blow to the head. But you are just plain crazy to go out in this cold."

"We'll be fine," Chris assured her with good humor. "Besides, you've got enough clothes here to keep four people warm."

"And you'll wear every piece," Mabel exclaimed, wrapping a scarf tightly around Julie's neck. "I'm not about to nurse any case of pneumonia. I've got enough to do around here without needing to nurse any fools."

Minutes later, feeling like a tightly wrapped mummy, Julie followed Chris out the back door. "You realize if I fall, I'll never be able to pull myself up again," she declared, her footsteps short and choppy as she struggled to keep her balance and not walk out of Mabel's too-big boots.

"At least if you fell, you'd make a terrific, heavenly angel," he observed, only his eyes visible above the red scarf that covered his nose and mouth.

"A fat little snow angel," Julie said with an unaccustomed grin, patting the layer of clothes that gave her shape a rotund appearance.

"Well, I'll be damned," he replied, pulling down the scarf to expose the rest of his face.

"What?" she asked.

"You can smile. I was really beginning to wonder."

"Of course I can smile," she retorted irritably. "It...it just hurts my forehead when I do," she added.

He looked at her for a long moment, as if attempting to probe her inner depths. She flushed warmly beneath the intensity of his gaze. "I'll say one thing. You're definitely easy on the eyes when you smile," he said, then turned and started walking once again.

Julie trudged after him, irritated that for just a moment his compliment had pleased her. Drat the man anyway, for being so...so...male. And double drat her for responding to him like a love-starved female.

She stomped after him, following him through the big barn door. Immediately she heard the stomping of horse hooves, smelled the scent of fresh hay, the pungent richness of worn leather.

"It will just take me a few minutes to hook up the boys," he said, upending a large bucket. "Why don't you sit right here and I'll come and get you when we're ready."

She nodded and sat down on the bucket, looking around as he disappeared into the stalls. She could hear him sweet-talking the horses, his voice soothing and gentle as he led them out of the stalls. She got up and went back to the barn door, gazing out over the whitened landscape. Once again, she found herself curious as to where, unintentionally, she had landed herself.

The Christmas motif was not just confined to the interior of the house—it spilled outside, as well. The front porch sported two huge columns, each one painted with red-and-white stripes to look like gigantic candy canes. Huge pine wreaths decorated with red ribbons hung on the window shutters and a silver garland was draped over the front door.

Granted, the man might just like Christmas, but she had a feeling it was more than that. Mabel had referred to the place as the North Pole, and she was positive she'd seen a reindeer outside her bedroom window.

Chris Kringle...that couldn't be his real name, she thought, sitting back down on the overturned bucket. *Surely that's just what he calls himself...a nickname,* she thought.

"We're all hooked up and ready to roll," Chris said as he appeared back in the doorway.

She got up and followed him through the side door of the barn, where outside the gleaming red sleigh awaited. The horses pawed the ground, blowing steam out their nostrils as they danced in anticipation.

Chris jumped up in the driver's seat, then held out his hand to help her up. Once she was seated next to him, he covered their laps with a thick blanket. Then, with a shake of the reins, they took off, gliding across the sparkling snow.

Although the bracing wind stung her cheeks slightly and her toes had passed from cold to numb, there was also an exhilaration as she smelled the crisp air, heard the sleigh bells ringing their tinkling voices, felt the reassuring warmth of Chris's firm thigh against her own.

As they headed out a set of front gates, Julie noticed a fenced-in area where several reindeer raised their heads at the sleigh's passing. At the same time they passed beneath a huge sign that read North Pole: Home Of Santa.

"Exactly what is this place?" she asked Chris, noticing how the wind had whipped ruddy color in his cheeks, only adding to his attractiveness.

"The North Pole," he answered, a teasing twinkle in his eyes.

"I know that . . . but is this your home, or what?"

"My home, my work, my dreams . . . my life." He smiled at her confusion. "The North Pole is a tourist attraction. We entertain hundreds of kids each year."

"Entertain how?"

"We've got the workshop with the elves making Santa's toys. There's a petting zoo with a menagerie of friendly four-legged creatures. Mabel cooks up dozens of Christmas cookies and barrels of hot chocolate, and we sing carols and tell stories. Then, of course, the visits end with a talk to the jolly red-suited man himself." He grinned at her. "Chris Kringle himself."

Julie scrunched her toes up in the oversize boots, seeking any warmth that might be hidden in the toes. "Chris Kringle . . . that's not your real name, is it?"

"Oh, but it is." He pulled on the reins, slowing the horses' gait to a leisurely walk. "My parents were Ed and Sarah Kringle, and they possessed a sense of humor I didn't always appreciate as a child.''

"You were teased a lot?"

"Mercilessly. For years, the kids at school would ask me where my reindeer were, so when I got old enough, I decided to stop fighting it. I bought nine reindeer and made my life's work portraying my namesake.''

"You don't look much like Santa Claus,'' Julie observed, now finding it difficult to believe that she'd ever mistaken this virile, overwhelmingly masculine man for the jolly old imp.

"Ah, but you haven't seen me in my red suit with my beard and hair sprayed white.'' He pulled hard on the reins as they descended a hill. "Your car should be someplace right in here,'' he explained when they'd neared the bottom of the rise.

"There...'' Julie pointed. The only thing visible was the top of the red hood that was crumpled upward. The rest of the car was covered in snow. Chris pulled the sleigh to a halt and together they jumped down and approached the wreck.

Julie moaned as she brushed the white powder away from the point of impact and saw the damage to the car. The front end was smashed, and the windshield glass looked like cracked eggshell.

She shivered, realizing that if Chris hadn't stumbled upon her, she probably would have frozen to death. She wrapped her arms around herself, watching as he pulled the driver door open and took the keys from the ignition. He then opened the trunk and removed her large suitcase. "Is this all you have?" he asked.

She nodded and he placed the keys beneath the floor mat in the driver's side. As they got back up on the sleigh and began the drive back, despair washed over Julie once again.

She had somehow hoped that he'd exaggerated the condition of the car. She'd hoped that when they reached it, she would find the fender bent, maybe the hood buckled a bit, but that the vehicle would be drivable. She'd wanted to be able to jump into the car and continue her trek to Kathy's isolated cabin, to escape the Christmas spirit that permeated Chris's house. She now realized that was impossible.

"Are you all right?" Chris asked after a moment of her silence. He looked at her, noting how the cold air had colored her cheeks, making the brown of her eyes even darker, richer. But he also noticed that her eyes were those of a lost soul, without spirit, without energy. Again he wondered what had happened in her life to cause the pain he sensed inside her.

"I'm fine," she replied, shivering slightly and pulling her scarf more tightly around her neck.

"Cold?" He moved closer to her, feeling the warm press of her thigh against his as he arranged the blanket closer around her.

"Really, I'm fine," she protested, moving her leg away from the heat of his.

He shook the reins, urging the horses faster as he felt the bite of the cold more vividly than he had moments before.

He glanced back at her, able to tell that she'd crawled someplace deep inside herself. There was something about the dispirited slump of her shoulders, the lackluster stare of her eyes that made him want to touch her, shake her . . . make her respond to him on a human level.

She was a beautiful woman, but he now found himself wondering how she would look in laughter. Would her eyes lighten to the color of caramel? Would the sound of it be low and rich, or high-pitched and girlish? Suddenly, more than anything else, he wanted to hear her laugh, but he had a feeling she found that particular expression difficult, and again he wondered what tragedy had stolen her laughter away from her.

He smiled at his own thoughts. Mabel would tell him he was crazy, imagining sorrow in everyone's eyes. But Chris had always been especially sensitive to others' pain. His mother had called it his gift, but there were times he thought it a curse.

He looked back at her and sighed. Whatever it was that haunted her, it really wasn't any of his business. He had other things to think about. This was his busiest time of the year. All he needed on his mind was spreading goodwill and cheer to the kids who came to the North Pole to see Santa.

Pulling the sleigh to a halt in front of the house, he jumped out and extended his hand to help her. As she reached out her hand to take his, he changed his mind and instead grabbed her by the waist and swung her down. Before he could set her firmly on the ground, both of Mabel's boots fell off Julie's feet and plopped into the snow.

With a burst of laughter, Chris pulled her back up into his arms before her stocking feet could touch the ground. Her breath was warm on his face and her eyes were widened in surprise. Her body tensed and quivered in his embrace.

"I . . . I can walk," she protested. "The door isn't that far away and I have on three pairs of socks."

"Oh, no, you don't," he exclaimed. "You aren't going to do that to me."

"What?" she asked, her brow wrinkled charmingly.

"You aren't going to make me put you down so you can run inside in your stocking feet and make Mabel yell at me for the next month."

She smiled, causing a dimple to appear at the corner of her mouth like a surprise package. "It might be worth a case of pneumonia just to see that."

"Ah, you're a wicked woman, Julie Casswell." He carried her to the front door and gently deposited her just inside. "I'll get Mabel's boots and your suitcase."

As he turned to walk back out into the snow, he felt warmer, and a cheerful whistle escaped his lips. Julie Casswell. She definitely intrigued him.

Her smile had been beautiful, a testimony that someplace deep inside her was a warm woman who'd once been on intimate terms with laughter, with life.

She was like a blooming flower encased in ice. Despite the resolution he'd made moments before to stay out of her life, her problems, he hoped she would be here long enough for him to try to melt the protective barrier she'd erected between herself and the rest of the world. He had a feeling the end result would be worth his efforts.

Chapter Four

"Ah, my patient is looking much better." The white-haired man arose from the table as Julie entered the kitchen for supper that evening.

"You must be Doc Rogers," she said. "I don't think we were officially introduced when Chris brought me in."

The old man smiled. "I rarely get officially introduced to my patients. Usually a lick on the hand is about all I can expect."

"How about a heartfelt thank-you instead?" Julie offered.

"No reason for thanks. I didn't do that much." He eyed the bruise on her forehead critically. "It's quite an attractive shade of purple, and I'd say you've got a few more colors to get through before it's completely gone. Are you feeling all right? No more dizziness or nausea?''

Julie shook her head. "No, I feel just fine." She turned and looked at Mabel, who was busy setting serving plates on the table. "Mabel, is there something I can do to help?"

"She never lets anyone help her in the kitchen," Doc explained. "She's downright stingy when it comes to her kitchen."

"Hrumph, I *have* to be stingy," Mabel retorted. "If I gave you and Chris full rein in here, you'd never eat a balanced meal, and I'd never get the mess cleaned up." She smiled at Julie. "Just sit down, honey. Everything should be ready in a minute or two." She motioned to the chair where Julie should sit.

Julie sat down and Doc joined her. "Where's Chris?" she asked.

"He's working out in the shed, trying to get the stage all ready," Doc explained.

"Stage?" Julie looked at him curiously.

"The shed is our little theater where every year the kids put on a Christmas play," Mabel said as she set a bowl of fried potatoes on the table. "This year, Chris decided to build a real stage for the kids."

Mabel's eyes twinkled brightly. "They're going to be so excited when they see it."

"It's even got curtains and floodlights and everything," Doc added proudly.

Julie slowly digested this bit of information, her heart pounding with rebellion. Kids and Christmas plays... The very thought sent a shaft of grief through her heart.

This thought was interrupted, though, as Chris entered through the back door. "Ah, good. I'm just in time," he said as Mabel set a huge sliced ham in the center of the table.

"You're always just in time," Mabel replied, then grinned at Julie. "From the time he was a little boy, he always seemed to know instinctively when I was putting the meal on the table."

Chris quickly shed his outer clothes and snow-covered boots, carefully placing them outside the back door, then joined them all at the table.

They waited until Mabel had sat down, then began passing the platters of food.

"Mmm, this all looks delicious," Julie said as she filled her plate. "If I'm not careful, I'll gain ten pounds before they get my car fixed and I'm on my way."

"You could stand to gain ten pounds," Mabel commented, patting her own plump tummy. "Unlike me."

"I like a woman with a little meat on her bones," Doc said, grinning at Mabel, who waved her napkin to dismiss him.

"I called Charley about your car," Chris interjected. "He said he'd try to get it towed in tomorrow if they have the roads cleared off enough. He's going to call and give you an estimate on the repairs."

Julie nodded, hoping whatever the repairs were, they wouldn't be too expensive and they wouldn't take too long.

"You might want to visit with Vixen. She wasn't acting quite right this afternoon, hasn't eaten much for the past two days, so I put her in a stall for observation," Doc said to Chris. "I don't think it's anything serious, but I thought it best to isolate her from the others."

"I'll check on her right after supper," Chris said.

The rest of the dinner conversation was pleasant, revolving around the weather and various work that still needed to be accomplished in the next couple of days.

Julie realized that running a place like the North Pole required a real commitment of time and money.

Again she found her gaze wandering to Chris, wondering what sort of man spent his life playing Santa Claus.

After dinner Chris invited Julie to the barn to check on the ailing reindeer. Once again they donned their outerwear and trudged outside, where the sun was just setting, giving the snow a rich, golden shine.

"It sounds like Mabel has worked for you for a long time," Julie said as they walked toward the barn.

"There are days when I'm not sure who works for whom," Chris replied with a laugh. "Mabel worked for my parents as a housekeeper until their deaths six years ago. When I opened this place five years ago, I contacted her to see if she wanted to work for me. She's one of my most favorite people in the whole world."

"She seems very kind."

Again Chris laughed, his eyes sparkling a deep shade of blue in the deepening twilight. "She's crusty on the outside, but she has a heart of gold."

"What about Doc? How long has he been here?"

"I hired Doc a year ago when I decided to incorporate the petting zoo. He'd recently retired, had no family to keep him busy and needed something to believe in once again. He found it here, helping me."

He opened the barn door and gestured for her to go on in. "Come on. She'll be in one of the stalls back here."

Julie followed him through the mazelike interior of the barn, going by stalls filled with sweet-smelling hay, and others where horses stomped and whinnied a welcome as they passed.

Chris stopped at the last stall where a reindeer immediately greeted him, nuzzling the hand he held out. "Hey, girl, what's the matter?" He spoke softly to the animal, scratching her beneath her chin as she gazed at him with her liquid brown eyes. "You can pet her," Chris urged Julie.

Julie reached out and lightly stroked the top of Vixen's nose. "I never knew they were so tame," she said, marveling.

"They're very easy to train and become quite sociable. They're like most creatures. They thrive on love." He smiled at Julie and gave the animal a final pat. "She'll probably be all right. Maybe she just needed a little extra attention."

As they walked back to the house, Julie looked up at the man next to her. He was unusual—so masculine, yet with a spirit so gentle, he drew old people and animals alike to him. She now noted how the soft dusk light painted his dark hair with gleaming highlights, how the approaching evening shadows emphasized the strength of his firm jaw, the sensual fullness of his mouth. Santa Claus...*hardly.* "Whatever made you decide to open a place like this?" she asked him. "Aside from the obvious reason of your name?"

He shrugged his broad shoulders. "My folks owned this land and had never done anything with it. There was a small cabin here, but not much of anything else."

He paused just outside the door to the house, his gaze lingering first on her, then encompassing the entire area. "I have a lot of wonderful Christmas memories from my childhood, and I guess there came a time in my life when I decided I wanted to make some memories for others, as well." He opened the door and Julie was grateful that the conversation had ended. She didn't want to hear about his wonderful Christmas memories. She didn't want to think of her own memories, now tainted and much too painful.

"How about a cup of hot chocolate for you two?" Mabel greeted them as they stepped into the kitchen.

"Sounds terrific," Chris replied, helping Julie off with her coat. She nodded, the beverage smelling delicious as it warmed in a pan on the top of the stove.

Moments later she and Chris sat at the table, sipping the hot cocoa. Mabel had disappeared, telling them she had work upstairs. "I can't remember the last time I drank hot chocolate that didn't come in a packet," Julie said, savoring the sweetness of the marshmallow-topped drink.

"Ah, Mabel considers instant hot cocoa nothing short of sacrilegious."

Julie noticed the way the marshmallow and chocolate decorated his upper lip, and for a moment she wondered how his mustache would feel in a kiss. Soft? Scratchy? The thought, so alien, so completely unexpected, threw her for a moment. She quickly averted her gaze, staring instead at the cheerful red gingham wallpaper behind him.

"We're going to decorate the big tree in the great room later this evening," he said, using a napkin to remove the traces of the drink from his mouth. "You're welcome to join us. We can always use another hand in draping tinsel and hanging ornaments."

"Oh, thanks, but I think I'll probably just make it an early night." Her heart positively clutched at the thought of helping them deck the halls and decorate the tree. She knew she couldn't make everyone else in the world stop celebrating Christmas, but that didn't mean she had to be a part of any celebration.

"More hot chocolate?" he asked, getting up from the table and moving over to the stove.

"No...no, thank you. I think I'll just head up to bed." She quickly finished the last of her drink, then got up and carried her cup to the sink. "I guess the fresh air of the sleigh ride this afternoon sapped all my energy." With a tight smile, she said good-night and hurried up to the bedroom that was quickly becoming her only retreat in this house filled with Christmas.

Once there, she ran a tub full of hot water in the adjoining bathroom, then eased herself into it, letting the warm water caress away the tension in her muscles.

She lay her head back against the cold porcelain of the tub, thinking about that moment when she'd wondered how it would be to kiss Chris. How could she even entertain the thought? Where on earth had it come from?

She sighed, realizing that what she'd told Chris about the fresh air sapping her energy was true. She was tired...tired of fighting her memories of the past, tired of anticipating the emptiness of her future. With a deep, weary sigh, she fell asleep.

She awoke sometime later, her bathwater cold and her body aching from the uncomfortable position it was in. She got out and dried off, then slipped into her nightgown and robe, grateful to have her own things to wear.

She'd spent most of the afternoon unpacking her clothes and things from the suitcase. She now lay down on the bed and picked up one of the paperback books she'd brought with her to help her pass the time at Kathy's cabin.

The catnap she'd had in the tub had lasted just long enough to refresh her and make sleep elusive.

She opened the book and tried to lose herself in the words on the pages, but sounds kept interfering with her concentration. The noise drifted up the stairs and through her door, pulling at her, encouraging her to investigate the merriment.

Finally, unable to ignore the sounds any longer, she slammed the book shut and got off the bed. With a dreadful reluctance, but unable to stop herself, she opened her door and went out into the hallway where the sound of frivolity wrapped itself around her.

She had only intended to watch for a moment or two, not wanting to join them, but was unable to resist the pull of their laughter. However, as she paused at the top of the stairs, Chris spied her and hurried over.

"Julie, come and join us," he urged. "We need an unbiased mediator."

"A referee, that's what we need," Doc added. "Mabel thinks she's the only one here who knows how to properly decorate the tree."

Mabel glared at the old man. "You might know what medicine will cure an ailing animal, but you don't know diddly about decorating a tree."

Julie allowed Chris to lead her over to a comfortable chair next to the tree, where she sank down into the softness as he soothed the others. "Now, now, we're doing fine," he said. "We've got all the lights strung and that's the most difficult part."

As Julie watched, Chris climbed up a ladder. Doc handed him colorful ornaments and he began to hang them on the uppermost branches of the huge tree. Mabel worked on the lower branches, stopping every moment or two to step back and offer her artistic comments on Chris's efforts.

"You've got too many red ones all bunched together," Mabel exclaimed, hands on her hips as she eyed the tree. "Maybe if you put a blue one there... No, then you'll have too many blue ones all together."

"Mabel, there are only so many colors we have to work with here," Chris replied, his tone holding the infinite patience of a man who'd been through this many times before.

"Well, put one of the silver bells up there." She grunted in satisfaction as Chris did as she asked.

As Julie watched them dressing the tree in its holiday finery, she remembered how much Livvy had always loved to decorate their white-flocked tree.

They always officially began the Christmas season on Thanksgiving Day, pulling out the tree and working on it while they digested the turkey-and-stuffing feast Julie always prepared.

Livvy and Julie had worked much the way Chris and Mabel did, with Julie doing the upper branches as Livvy took care of the ones her little arms could reach.

"Look, Momma, look," Livvy would say after each ornament she hung, and dutifully, Julie would step back and exclaim over what a perfect job Livvy had done.

The memory was so rich, so full of flavor that it surrounded Julie, encouraging her to pull forth another and another so she could be bathed in the light of Livvy. Livvy, singing the words to "Silent Night," her brow puckered in concentration. Livvy, silver tinsel on top of her head, proclaiming herself a Christmas tree. Livvy, cuddled against Julie's side on the sofa in the living room, the colorful lights of the tree dancing reflectively in her big brown eyes. "Just a smidgen longer, Momma," she would beg when it was bedtime, and always, Julie had let her stay up just a smidgen longer.

Julie hugged the precious visions to her, wanting them to go on and on forever, needing them to insulate her from the harshness of her present reality. They wrapped her in love and warmth.

"Julie, are you all right?"

As if from a distance, Julie heard Chris's voice. She snapped her head up, angry at the interruption, then realizing where she was, she focused her attention and saw him perched atop the ladder, holding a beautiful white-and-silver angel in his hands.

"I...yes..." But she wasn't all right. Pain shot through her heart, the ugly cold pain of bereavement, her lonely, aching, constant companion. She stood up, almost reeling beneath the weight of her emotions. "I...I have to go." Barely conscious of their surprised looks, she ran up the stairs to the bedroom. She was vaguely aware of Chris calling after her, but she didn't stop her upward flight, wanting only to be alone with her grief.

She knew better than to allow herself memories. It only made it so much more difficult when she crawled out of those visions from the past.

She whirled around as her bedroom door opened. Chris stood in the doorway. "Julie, are you all right?"

She nodded, for a moment not trusting herself to speak.

He took several steps toward her, standing so close she could see the tiny flecks of gold that speckled his blue irises. She swallowed hard, disciplining her emotions as she had so many times in the past. "I'm fine."

"I don't think so," he countered, taking another step toward her, standing so close that the warmth radiating from his body seemed to envelop hers. "Talk to me, Julie. Tell me what's wrong." His voice was softly persuasive, rich with concern, rippling over her like precious water on a parched throat.

She leaned toward him, knowing that his arms would offer her comfort, that she could lose herself and her pain in his embrace. Yet how could she think of her own comfort? How could she even consider easing her own pain?

She backed away from him, suddenly angry with him and his festive home, angry with the Fates that had placed her here. "All I need is to be left alone." She drew her robe more tightly around her, as if it could shield her from him and his caring eyes. "I just want to be left alone," she repeated more forcefully.

He stood for a long moment, his eyes searching hers as if he could glean the inner workings of her soul if he merely looked long enough, hard enough.

Finally he gave her a small nod. "Then I guess I'll just say good-night." With that, he turned and left the room, gently closing the door behind him.

Julie expelled a tremulous sigh when he was gone, her legs trembling as she made her way over to the bed. She was cold...so cold. She didn't remove her robe, but instead crawled right in beneath the covers, praying only that the oblivion of sleep would claim her quickly.

"Is she all right?" Mabel asked worriedly as Chris came back downstairs.

Chris shrugged helplessly, a frown furrowed on his forehead. "She says she is, but I don't know." He thought about the expression on her face as she'd watched them decorating the tree. It had been obvious when he'd looked at her that she was far away.

When he'd called to her, her expression had changed from glowing happiness to one of frantic horror, wild anxiety. What had she been thinking about? he wondered. What pictures had she been seeing in her mind?

"Maybe she just had a headache," Doc offered, his eyes also filled with concern. "That bruise is probably still pretty painful."

"That was no headache," Mabel objected, clucking her tongue softly as she opened another box of brightly colored tree ornaments. "That woman's got a misery... a deep misery of the heart."

A misery of the heart—yes, that was exactly what Chris thought. Something that was keeping her isolated, distanced from the life that was going on around her.

Although Chris had always viewed Christmas as a celebration of love, a renewal of the human spirit, he knew that there were some people who had trouble facing the holidays. He was aware that this was a time of tremendous stress and anxiety for many.

He thought again of the look in Julie's dark brown eyes, of the expression of pain so deep, it had cut through him, piercing his own heart in sympathy.

"Time... that's the only thing that heals that sort of misery," Mabel muttered, once again working on the tree.

Chris joined her, his mind whirling with possibilities. Yes, time was a great healer, but so was the spirit of Christmas. He had a feeling that if he could keep her here for a little while, he might be able to break through the barrier of tight control she had wrapped around herself. He might be able to lance her wound and drain the cancerous pain that prevented her from reaching out to anyone for anything.

Time. Yes, that was exactly what he needed. Just a little bit of time. For some reason the thought of Julie leaving here and going to an isolated cabin to spend Christmas Eve frightened him. Nobody should be alone on Christmas Eve, especially not a woman whose eyes held an indefinable sorrow powerful enough to dim the light of her soul.

If only there was some way to keep her here until after Christmas Eve.... He smiled as a thought suddenly crossed his mind. He probably shouldn't even consider it—it would be a shameless manipulation of fate. He really didn't have the right to do such a thing.

But as he thought of the brief smile she'd given him earlier in the day, as he remembered the way she'd unconsciously leaned toward him even as her words told him to leave her alone, he realized someplace deep inside of her was a part that was crying out for help. Could he help her? Should he even consider it?

"I think that does it. Chris, you want to get the lights?" Mabel said, putting the last of the silver tinsel on the tree.

He nodded and moved to the switch on the wall. As he shut off the overhead lights, Doc plugged in the twinkling colorful ones of the tree.

Immediately the tree came to life, the sight never failing to steal Chris's breath away momentarily. It was amazing what some lights and tinsel could do to an ordinary evergreen tree. It just took a little time and a little energy to transform a tree. What would it take to transform Julie?

As he stood staring at the glory of the sight, he contemplated the woman upstairs and came to a final decision. He would call Charley at the garage first thing in the morning.

As the decision completed itself in his mind, he had the sudden, distinct impression that the smile on the angel's face at the very top of the tree had widened.

Chapter Five

Julie awoke to the sound of heavy machinery in the distance. Jumping out of bed, she ran over to the window and peered out. She breathed a sigh of relief as she saw the bright yellow grader followed by a lumbering sand truck making slow progress on the distant road.

Good. She turned away from the window with a grateful sigh. If they cleared the roads this morning, then Charley should have her car in the shop by noon. She'd be on her way to Kathy's cabin in the next day or two.

She dressed quickly, choosing a rust colored sweater and a pair of brown slacks. Brushing her hair, she thought about what had happened the night before and realized she owed Chris an apology. She knew the way she'd abruptly run from the living room had concerned him, and she'd met his concern with rudeness.

She shoved away thoughts of the night before, refusing to allow herself to dwell on the memories that had filled her so completely, then left her so bereft.

She ran lightly down the stairs, her nose immediately assailed with the luscious scents of cinnamon and spice, apples and baking chocolate. "Mmm, something smells wonderful," she said as she entered the kitchen, where Mabel had just pulled a tray out of the oven.

"Cookies," Mabel explained. "I've been working on them all morning. I've got chocolate-chip cookies, sugar cookies, apple jam bars and gingerbread. We've got two busloads of kids scheduled for this afternoon and it looks like they'll manage to get here."

Julie helped herself to a cup of coffee. "Yes, I saw the road workers out clearing off the snow." She sat down at the table and watched as Mabel dropped a dozen more dollops of dough on the cookie sheet then popped the tray back into the oven. With the back of one arm, she pushed a few stray strands of hair off her forehead, her face flushed from the heat of her baking.

"It's not even nine o'clock yet, and you already look pooped," Julie observed.

Mabel grinned and refilled her coffee cup. "I've been up since a little after five. I wanted to get an early start on these cookies. The kids go through stacks of them."

Julie stared toward the window thoughtfully, thinking of this house filled with children. It was a daunting thought. She'd been very careful in the past year to keep herself isolated from children, finding their laughter, their smiling little faces too painful to be around. How was she going to get through a day of seeing kids everywhere?

"Did you sleep well?" Mabel asked, joining her at the table.

"Like a log." She smiled at Mabel. "I can't thank you enough for all your hospitality while I've been here. Hopefully I'll be out of your hair in the next day or two."

Mabel leaned forward and patted Julie's hand. "Sugar, you haven't been in anybody's hair. This house loves people, and if Chris had his way, he'd have it filled with kids and people all the time."

"He seems very nice."

"Chris is just short of a saint, in my eyes." Mabel smiled softly. "He's got a heart that sometimes outweighs his common sense. 'Course I'd never let him know how I feel." She stopped talking as the buzzer on the oven rang shrilly. Jumping up, she grabbed a hot pad mitten and took the golden brown cookies out of the oven. "How about some breakfast?" she asked.

Julie shook her head. "No, thanks. I'm really not much of a breakfast eater. This coffee is just fine." She sipped from her cup, watching as Mabel prepared another baking sheet to go into the oven.

She wanted to hear more about Chris. Had he ever been married? What kind of a childhood had he experienced? What would his strong arms feel like wrapped around her? This last thought brought a flush of warmth to her face. Where on earth had that come from? she wondered incredulously.

At that moment Chris walked in, and she felt the blush intensify.

"Good morning." He greeted the two women cheerfully, grabbing one of the oven-warmed cookies and scooting away before Mabel's playful backhand could connect. "Our first busload of kids should be here in about thirty minutes."

"So soon?" Mabel squeaked, pulling out another baking tray from a cabinet. "I'd better get these finished up and get into my holiday clothes." She looked at Chris. "Hadn't you better get into your things?"

"It'll just take me a few minutes to hop into the suit. Since you're finishing up the cookies, perhaps Julie will help me spray my hair."

"Spray your hair?" She looked at him blankly.

"Make it white," he explained. "I can get most of it, but I always need help in the back."

"Okay, sure I'll help," she replied, consciously pushing aside her disturbing thoughts of moments before.

"Great! Then I guess I'd better head up and get into the suit. I'll call you when I'm ready for your help." He started to leave, then reached back and grabbed another of the cookies, laughing as Mabel shooed him out of the kitchen.

Minutes later as Julie headed back up to her room, Chris called to her. She followed the sound of his voice, surprised to realize his bedroom was the one right next to hers. It was distinctly masculine. The bed was king-size with a massive, rich walnut headboard. The spread and curtains were desert colors, browns and cactus greens. She would have known it was Chris's bedroom by the scent. The entire room smelled the same way he did, like fresh evergreen and falling snow and clean mountain winds.

"Chris?" she said tentatively, pausing just inside the doorway, not seeing him anywhere around. His Santa suit was on the bed, ready to be donned. "Chris?" she repeated a little louder.

He stuck his head out of an adjoining doorway and smiled at her, his mustache and beard already a startling white. "If you could just give me a hand in the back," he said, motioning her into the spacious bathroom, where he stood before a large wall mirror.

Julie nodded, her mouth dry as she moved closer to where he stood. He was bare-chested, clad only in a pair of tight jeans. Draped around his neck was a towel that did nothing to hide the linear lines of the muscles of his upper arms, the natural bronze coloring of his chest and back.

"What...what do you want me to do?" she asked, hoping her voice didn't sound as breathless as she suddenly felt.

"Let's go in here where there's more room."

She nodded, following him into the bedroom, grateful to be out of what had suddenly seemed to be the small confines of the bathroom. The temperature had been at least ten degrees warmer in there.

He sat down sideways on the edge of the bed. "If you could just spray the back of my hair," he explained, handing her the spray can.

Again she nodded and stepped up closer to him, shaking the can vigorously, trying to keep her mind off how smooth, and how warm his skin looked. She managed to spray most of the dark strands without touching him in any way.

However, in order to get the hair around his ears and at the nape of his neck, she had to lean closer and brace herself by placing one hand on one of his broad shoulders.

Just as she'd suspected, his flesh was warm and supple beneath her fingertips. She'd forgotten how pleasant the sensation of touching another human being could be. She tilted his head slightly to get the last of the darkness, realizing that even with hair the color of newly fallen snow, he was still devastatingly handsome.

His dark hair made his eyes seem tremendously blue, but with the shock of white, they appeared to be almost silver in hue. "I think that's it," she murmured, looking closely for any telltale darkness amid the white.

Before she could step back, he stood up, the movement bringing him achingly close to her. For a moment she couldn't move. She felt trapped by his nearness, by his evocative scent that infused her. She was momentarily mesmerized by the warmth emanating from his eyes. She saw life there, and the kind of spontaneous laughter she'd once had.

As if in a dream, she saw his hand reach up, felt the softness of his fingertips as they brushed first against the bruise on her forehead, then trailed down the side of her face.

She closed her eyes, lost in a maelstrom of emotions at the tactile pleasure. It had been so long, so very long since she'd allowed herself to be touched in any way. His fingers were warm silk wrapped around a core of strength, evoking in her a longing she had denied for what seemed like a lifetime.

"Julie." Her name was a soft whisper on his lips and as she opened her eyes and gazed at him, she realized the color of his eyes had changed, deepening and now reflecting heat and flames.

The desire, so naked in his eyes, shocked her, pulled her out of the fog that had surrounded her. She stepped back from him at the same moment a horn blared outside the window.

"What...what's that?" she asked, grateful for the interruption that effectively broke the spell of the moment.

"That's the bus," he said, reluctantly reaching for his Santa suit.

Julie nodded. "I'll just let you finish getting dressed." She ran from his room and into hers, her body trembling uncontrollably.

She sat down on the bed and wrapped her arms around herself, trying to still the convulsive shivering that assailed her from head to toe.

What had he done to her? Even as the question made its way into her mind, she knew the answer. He'd made her feel again. For a brief moment, while his fingers had played their magic along the side of her face, he'd managed to penetrate through the protective shield she'd erected around herself a year ago.

She cocked her head slightly, suddenly aware of a sound drifting through her window. She got up, and on wooden legs walked across the room, pulling aside the curtains and peering outside.

Kids. They were everywhere, their brightly colored coats beacons against the pristine snow, their voices ringing out in laughter. She leaned her head against the cold glass. She knew it was insanity, she knew it was irrational, but she checked each and every child's face, looking for a little girl she knew she wouldn't find.

Pain lanced through her with an intensity that threatened to crumple her. The children's colored coats and smiling faces all ran together, blurred by the mist of her tears.

She remembered now why she didn't allow herself to feel. It hurt too much. She needed her shield. It protected her against the pain.

She swiped her tears angrily, vowing that she would not, could not, allow Chris, with his kind blue eyes and warm touch, to get beneath it again.

Julie remained in her room all day, trapped by the sounds of childish laughter, the merry Christmas carol singing, the happy voices that rose and fell like swelling scales played on a piano. She tried to read, but found she couldn't concentrate on the words, couldn't focus on the meaning.

She paced the length and width of the room, feeling like a prisoner, yet knowing that her imprisonment was self-imposed.

Just when she thought she couldn't stand it any longer, just when she thought if she heard one more burst of laughter, one more song of joy, she would go quite mad, they left.

It was early evening when she finally ventured out of her room, driven by hunger and lulled by the silence of the house.

She crept down the stairs, carefully keeping her eyes averted from the huge Christmas tree. The empty kitchen greeted her and she went directly to the refrigerator, somehow knowing nobody would mind if she fixed herself a sandwich or some leftovers.

Spying the remains of their ham dinner from the night before, she made herself a sandwich and poured a glass of milk, then sat down at the table.

As she ate, her mind replayed that strange moment in Chris's room, when she'd felt as if she'd been bewitched by the touch of his hand against the side of her face. It was really little wonder that she'd responded so quickly, so intensely. It had been almost six years since she'd been touched by a man's hand, six years since she'd shared an adult relationship, made love.

Tom. She wondered what had ever happened to him. He'd blown into her life like a hot whirlwind, and had snuck out of her life like a thief in the night. Their marriage had lasted exactly four months, until she'd told him she was pregnant. He'd gone to work one day and never returned. She'd received divorce papers in the mail two months later—that was the last she'd heard from him.

She wondered if he knew...if he would even care. She doubted it. He hadn't cared about Livvy's birth—why would he care about the fact that she was gone? Pushing away from the table, she cleaned up her mess and started to leave the kitchen, pausing as she saw the reflection of a light shining outside the back door. Curious, she peered out, cupping her hands on either side of her face to aid her vision in the darkness outside.

The light shone from inside the shed, and she suddenly remembered Doc and Mabel talking about a stage Chris was building. Her curiosity piqued, she grabbed one of the coats that hung on a rack by the back door and pulled it on. Adding Mabel's over-size boots, she stepped out the back door.

The snow crunched beneath her boots, its surface sparkling like diamond dust fallen from the sky. Overhead, the stars twinkled brightly, as if in competition with the glistening snow. Julie took deep breaths of the cold, evergreen-scented air, finding it invigorating, energizing.

The shed door opened without a sound, and Julie instantly realized she'd walked into a play rehearsal in progress. About a dozen children were onstage, several others running along the rows of wooden pews that formed the audience section.

Chris was onstage, his hair back to its normal dark luster. Julie sat down on one of the benches at the back, watching as he worked with the kids, telling them where to stand, what to say.

He was good with the children, infinitely patient, his facial muscles relaxed in an easy smile. Julie found herself studying him, noting the way he pulled on the side of his mustache when he thought, how often he patted one of the kids on the back or wrapped his arms around them in a hug. And it was obvious the children adored him.

"Hi."

Julie jumped at the sound of the voice next to her. She turned to see a young boy, perhaps no older than five or six. His round face was creased with a friendly smile as he gazed at Julie in the straightforward fashion children possess.

"Hi," she returned, stifling the automatic instinct to reach out and smooth down his tousled red hair.

"I'm Benjamin. What's your name?"

"Julie."

"Are you gonna be in the play?" he asked.

Julie shook her head. "No, I'm just watching."

His little chest expanded with pride. "I'm in the play. I'm one of the wise men." His blue eyes gazed at her solemnly, letting her know he took his role quite seriously. "I bring baby Jesus some Frankenstein."

Julie bit her bottom lip to trap the smile at his error. "I think it's frankincense," she corrected.

Strange how talking to him didn't bother her. *Perhaps it's because he's a boy,* she thought. *Not a sweet little girl like Livvy.*

"Oh, yeah, frankincense. That's right," he agreed. He scooted up on the bench next to her, bringing with him the special scent of childhood. "I've got a frog."

Julie blinked at the sudden change of topic. She'd forgotten how kids had a tendency to do that. "What's your frog's name?"

Benjamin looked up at the stage, a wide grin on his face. "Chris. My frog's name is Chris." He looked back at Julie. "Are you Chris's friend?"

"Sort of."

He swung his feet back and forth, as if following an internal rhythm only he could hear. "I'm one of Chris's extraspecial friends. He helped me catch my frog."

"Benjamin," Chris called from the stage, his surprise obvious when he saw Julie sitting beside the boy. "Come on, kiddo. I need you up here."

"I gotta go," Benjamin said to Julie, gifting her with a beatific smile. He slid off the bench and ran toward the stage.

Suddenly Julie needed to get out, get away. Benjamin's essence of life surrounded her, the smell of him haunted her, a childlike scent she wanted to wrap herself in.

She jumped up from the bench and ran to the door. Jerking it open, she stumbled out into the snow, the ice around her heart as cold as the blanket beneath her feet.

Tears rose in her throat, begging to be shed, but she refused to allow their release. She had yet to allow herself the luxury of a good, hard cry. She was afraid that once she began, she'd never be able to stop.

Once back inside the house, she carefully set Mabel's boots just outside the door, then hung the coat back on the rack. She walked out through the kitchen and paused at the great room, her gaze captured by the glory of the shimmering, lighted Christmas tree.

It was so beautiful. Without thought, drawn almost against her will, she sank down onto the sofa near the chair where she'd sat the night before when she'd watched the others decorating.

The brightly colored lights created reflections on each shiny ornament, and in each reflection Julie saw Livvy.

Julie wrapped her arms around herself, rocking back and forth against the pain, wanting to fall into the illusions that danced and shimmered on the tree.

Livvy had loved Christmas more than any child Julie had ever known. She'd been born on December 27, and it was as if the doctor had spanked the spirit of Christmas into her when he'd welcomed her into the world.

How could Julie enjoy another Christmas knowing her child never would? How could she get into the spirit of giving when the thing she loved the most had been so suddenly stolen from her?

Livvy should be here, sharing the magic of the North Pole. She should be here to pet the reindeer and be in the play. "She should be here for me," Julie whispered softly, her arms aching with the need to cradle, hug, enfold Livvy against her heart.

She had no idea how long she sat there, lost in the grief that was still so deep, it threatened to swallow her up. It could have been minutes, it might have been hours. She was lost in the silence of the house surrounding her, as she stared at the tree that was a painful reminder of all she had lost, yet embodied all that had been so good.

"Julie?"

She looked up and saw Chris standing in the doorway. He moved into the room and sat down beside her. "I just took all the kids home and was on my way up to bed when I saw you sitting here." He settled back, his gaze going to the tree. "It's beautiful, isn't it? There's something hypnotic about the lights on a tree. It's sort of like staring into a crackling fire. People see all kinds of images."

She nodded, not trusting herself to speak. The deep well of tears she had fought off for the past twelve months were suddenly ridiculously close to the surface. She was afraid that if she looked at him, uttered a single word, she would lose all control.

"Christmas is a difficult time for lots of people," Chris said softly. "Some see it as an end, and they use the time to reflect on what they've lost, all the sadness, all the negatives." He leaned closer to her, his hand reaching out to lightly touch one of hers. "I try to use this time of year to think of the coming year, the wonderful things I anticipate will happen. I always try to look ahead, not back."

Julie's insides clenched tightly and she turned and looked at him, defeated, knowing her internal agony was on her face for him to see. "And what do you do when your future looks as empty, as painful as anything you've ever experienced?"

"You talk about it. You share your fears with somebody else, you share your pain with somebody else."

"I can't." She stood up from the sofa, poised to run, needing to escape the kindness of his eyes, knowing her control was dangerously close to snapping.

Chris stood up, as well, and before she could turn and run, he reached out and gently pulled her into the embrace of his arms. "Talk to me, Julie," he breathed softly into her hair.

She shook her head, holding herself rigid against the warmth of his body. The heat of his embrace, the compelling feel of his arms wrapped around her, were like enemy-warrior battering rams beating against her defenses. She looked up at him, the image misting as tears filled her eyes.

"I...I can't...I must..." Her protests were weak and as he reached up and pressed his hand on the back of her head, guiding her cheek to the strength of his chest, Julie felt her control snap.

The deep, gut-wrenching tears she had denied herself for so long were suddenly there, pressing against her eyelids, oozing down her cheeks.

She was vaguely aware of Chris, his hands stroking her hair, his heartbeat loud and strong beneath her cheek, his voice low and soothing as he murmured in her ear. She clung to him, afraid of the depth of her grief even as she fell into it.

And then she was there, in a black hole where all she felt was her loss, all she thought of was the emptiness of her life. For the first time, she allowed her grief to consume her, sobs ripping through her as she clung desperately to Chris's strength.

"Hold me," she cried, afraid that if Chris let go of her, she would disappear into her anguish, lose herself in misery.

The intensity of her emotions frightened her, and she was somewhat relieved that Chris seemed to recognize her fear and respond to it, holding her so tight, she was afraid she would drown him in her tears.

She tried to struggle away from him, suddenly fearing she would infect him with her sorrow, fearful she might tarnish his optimism, his obvious love of life, with her pain. But he refused to allow her any distance, merely tightening the embrace that both comforted her and scared her.

Slowly, almost imperceptibly at first, her tears began to stop and she felt herself crawling up from the black void where she'd momentarily descended. Although sobs still convulsively jerked her body, her tears slowly dissipated, leaving behind a highly attuned sensitivity to Chris and her immediate surroundings.

His evocative scent enveloped her, infused her, filling her head with a new, different emotion. She was intensely aware of the length of his legs pressed tightly against hers, the intimate closeness of their hips fitted together. She could feel the muscles of his back and shoulders, so strong, so capable. Finally she was aware of his heartbeat resounding with a rapidity that stirred the beating of her own.

"Julie." His voice was deep and hoarse, compelling her to look up at him. His eyes were silvery blue, emanating a white fire that torched through her, centering in her very core.

She knew he was going to kiss her, and she wanted him to. She wanted his lips to stoke a fire in her so hot, so searing, that it would banish everything else from her mind. She tilted her mouth upward, parting her lips in conscious invitation.

With a deep moan, he captured her mouth with his, plying her lips with a heat that seeped throughout her entire being.

She welcomed the flames, opening her mouth to allow him to deepen the kiss. He did, his tongue stroking inside in bold demand. His hands moved up her back, slowly, sensually, up beneath the sweatshirt she wore, making her blood thicken like slow-flowing lava.

Julie fell into a different kind of dark hole, one where desire was the only emotion, a desire so intense it left no room for anything else. She wallowed in it, allowing it to coil in her stomach. She reveled in it, lost in the forgotten joy of it.

As he released her mouth, she dropped her head back, closing her eyes as his lips nipped and kissed the soft skin of her neck. She tangled her hands in his hair, loving the softness of the dark tendrils that wrapped around her fingers.

His mouth once again sought hers and as he kissed her, one of his hands remained on her back and the other one moved around to splay against her stomach. Pausing for a moment, as if waiting for a protest, his hand moved languidly upward, cupping her breast through the lacy material of her bra.

Julie's senses reeled at the sensation of her nipple rising up to meet the heat of his caress, and she arched against him, loving the way he stroked fire into every cell of her being.

As his mouth moved from her lips, across her jawline and toward her ear, she turned her head and opened her eyes, the Christmas tree filling her vision. And in the shining ornaments danced the vision of her little girl.

Gasping, surfacing from the desire that had obliterated everything else from her mind, she reeled back from him, appalled by what she'd allowed to take place.

She stared at Chris in horror, shocked that she'd allowed his caresses to make her forget about Livvy.

Guilt ripped through her...guilt that even for a brief instant she could forget about the little girl she'd lost.

He looked at her in obvious confusion, his eyes still lit with the flames that had so effectively pulled her in. "Julie?" He took a step toward her, but she stumbled away from him, her guilt ripping through her, tearing at her heart. How could she, for even a single, solitary moment, have forgotten Livvy? The desire she'd felt only moments before now seemed a direct affront to Livvy's memory.

"I'm...I'm sorry," she said. "This should have never happened...it's wrong. It's all wrong." Knowing it was an inadequate explanation, but unable to say anything more, she turned and ran up the stairs.

Chris stared after her, trying to bring his own emotions under control. He sank down on the sofa and raked a hand through his hair. What had begun as his attempt to comfort her had quickly escalated beyond anything he'd imagined. The desire that had flared between them had apparently caught her as much by surprise as it had him. In fact, it still sang through his body, rich and intense as he remembered the soft moistness of her lips, the satiny feel of her skin, the way she had arched herself against him.

If ever there was a woman made for loving, it was Julie. If ever there was a woman whose soul needed loving, it was Julie's. So what was it that kept her from reaching out? What tragedy in her life had stolen her will to live, made her consciously fight against her own needs, her very nature?

He stared at the twinkling tree, wondering how on earth he could find the answers she kept so close to her heart.

One thing was certain. Kissing her had been like embracing life. It had filled him with a sense of wonder and joy. He had a feeling that healing Julie's pain would be like opening the best Christmas present he'd ever received in his entire life. But how could he help her if she fought him every step of the way? What could he do to erase the shadows in her eyes?

He stared up at the angel atop the tree, but she didn't seem to have any answers, either.

Chapter Six

Julie knew that sooner or later she would have to go downstairs and face Chris. But she found herself lingering in her room, postponing the inevitable morning-after encounter between herself and the man who'd haunted her dreams all night long.

Even now, with the bright morning sunshine streaking through the window, the memory of those sensual dreams had the power to pull a heated blush to her cheeks.

She scoffed irritably, picking up her hairbrush and pulling it through her hair for the third time. She was twenty-five years old, far too old to indulge in adolescent nonsense.

"It was just a kiss or two," she said to her reflection. But even as she said it, she knew she was fooling herself. What she'd shared with Chris had been much more than a mere kiss or two. It had been a reawakening of something that had lain dormant for too long, a reemergence from the darkness into the warmth of the light.

But it was a transition she didn't want to make. She didn't want to crawl out of the darkness, not without Livvy by her side.

One thing was for certain. Whatever had happened between herself and Chris had been a mistake, a momentary lapse of strength on her part. It would definitely not be repeated.

With this conviction firmly in her heart, she left her room and headed down to the kitchen.

She'd just entered the cheerful room when the wall phone rang. Chris jumped up from the table where he was sitting with Doc and Mabel and answered the call, immediately holding the receiver out to her. "It's Charley from the garage."

Julie nodded, eagerly taking the receiver from him and greeting the mechanic. Her eagerness quickly turned to dismay as Charley outlined the damage to her car. It wasn't until he told her how long he anticipated the repairs to take that she voiced her anxiety. "A week!" she squealed into the receiver. "Surely you can do something before that?"

She listened impatiently as Charley explained to her the problems in obtaining a new radiator to replace her ruptured one. "Yes, I understand. Thank you." She hung up the phone and turned to face the others at the table. "I don't suppose there's another garage anywhere nearby, is there?"

All three shook their heads. "Charley's got the only place around these parts," Doc answered.

"Problems?" Chris asked.

Julie nodded, her gaze not quite meeting his. "Charley said he has to send to Denver for a new radiator and he says he has several cars ahead of mine. It will be at least a week before mine will be ready."

"Wonderful," Mabel exclaimed. "That means you'll be here to see our play and share all the Christmas Eve festivities."

"Surely it would be best if I just got a room at a nearby motel," Julie said.

"Nonsense," Mabel scoffed, rising from the table. "It would be sheer foolishness for you to go to a motel and be stuck in some room alone without a car. Besides—" she pointed at Chris and Doc "—the two of them are always ganging up on me. With you here, the odds are a little bit more in my favor."

Julie nodded, biting the inside of her mouth to suppress a grin. She had a feeling that Mabel had no problem holding her own, no matter how uneven the odds.

Having poured herself a cup of coffee, Julie joined Chris and Doc at the table. As she sipped from her cup, she shot a surreptitious glance at Chris. She noted the way the sunshine streaming in the window stroked the rich highlights of his dark hair, how it emphasized the bold strength of his features.

She flushed as his gaze suddenly caught hers. She quickly looked away, wondering how on earth she was going to manage to remain here for another seven days and not completely lose her sanity.

"As soon as I finish my coffee, I was going to try to get the train put together around the base of the tree," Chris announced. "Would you be interested in helping me?" He looked at her expectantly.

She knew she should decline. The last thing she wanted was to spend any time with him. But she also dreaded the thought of being cooped up all day in her room. Besides, what had happened between them last night had been brought on by his offer of comfort, by the weakness of her tears.

She'd been lost in her grief and that had made her vulnerable to his kisses. And she couldn't really fault him for kissing her. She'd wrapped herself around him like a ribbon on a package. It was no wonder one thing had led to another. It had merely been an accident of biology, a quick chemical reaction—nothing more.

"Julie?"

She flushed again, realizing he was waiting for her answer. "Sure, I'll help," she finally agreed, determined to maintain control. After all, she was stuck here with him for the next week or so. She couldn't very well spend the entire time in her room. Yes, she was stuck, but she was determined to make the best of things.

"Chris, Mr. Bailey called from the feed store," Mabel said as she poured them all another cup of coffee. "He wanted me to jiggle your memory concerning your account with him."

Chris slapped his palm down on the table before him. "I forgot all about those bills. I've got a whole stack of them on my desk. I'll get to them sometime this evening."

"Hmm...famous last words." Mabel clucked her tongue. "Someday they're going to come and close us down because you forgot to pay the bills. I swear, I've never known a man who has such an aversion to paperwork."

Chris stood up and drained his coffee cup, grinning at Julie. "Come on. Let's make a fast escape to the train. Otherwise I'm in for a lecture about my lack of business acumen.''

Julie followed him out of the kitchen and into the great room, her mind whirling with questions. Was the North Pole in financial trouble? Was he having a problem meeting expenses? Even though this place made her uncomfortable personally, it would be a shame if it had to close down. Even though she herself never would enjoy the spirit of Christmas, that didn't mean she wanted to steal the holiday away from the rest of the world. Still, she knew this was none of her business, and so the questions remained only in her mind.

Together they sat down at the base of the tree, where the train tracks were partially laid out, but unconnected. "It's really pretty easy to do," he explained, taking two pieces and showing her how to snap them together.

They worked for several minutes, Doc and Mabel's barely discernible voices coming from the kitchen, the clicking of the track pieces snapping together being the only sound in the room.

As she worked, she found that her gaze lingered again and again on Chris's hands. He had nice hands with long fingers. They looked strong, yet capable of gentleness. She knew they were warm. Vivid images of them stroking up the flesh of her back danced through her mind, bringing a flame of heat into the pit of her stomach.

"How long have you had the train?" she asked, desperate for a topic of conversation that would take her thoughts off other, more dangerous ones.

A smile curved his lips upward. "My parents bought me the original one when I was twelve years old. Since then I've replaced some of the parts and added pieces. But the locomotive is still the original one that chugged its way around the base of our Christmas tree twenty years ago."

He snapped the last length of track into place, completing the big circle around the base of the tree. He got up and grabbed two large boxes. He sat back down, one of the boxes beside him, the other next to her. "I've got the train. You've got the village."

"The village?" She reached into the box and pulled out a miniature Victorian home complete with lights at the windows and realistic-looking snow on the roof. "Oh, how wonderful," she exclaimed, marveling at the minute details and exquisite craftsmanship that had gone into the wooden piece. "These are beautiful," she said, pulling out another one, a bakery with various cakes and pies visible behind the glass window. "The workmanship is gorgeous."

"Thanks," he replied.

There was something in his tone of voice that made her look at him curiously. "Did you make these?"

He nodded, boyish pride shining from his eyes. "Even Santa Claus needs a hobby."

"What do you do around here when it isn't Christmastime?" she asked, watching as he unpacked the train. "I can't imagine you get many tourists in the middle of summer."

"You'd be surprised—Christmas is popular no matter what the season." He blew the dust off a miniature coal car and grinned at her.

"Then why don't you keep the train up all year-long?" she asked curiously.

He ran a finger slowly across the top of the black car, his smile soft and reflective. "There are some things that you don't share with all the tourists. This train is a part of my personal, special tradition, one I share only with my closest friends." He hooked the car behind the locomotive and smiled at her. "I'm glad you're here to share it with me."

"Thanks." She felt a warm blush cover her face and turned her concentration on unloading the rest of the miniature buildings. For the next few minutes they worked in silence, but it was a companionable one.

Each building she pulled out of the box heightened her admiration for Chris's talent. Not only were there houses and stores, but also people and trees, bridges and street lanterns. The box contained everything necessary to create a charming turn-of-the-century village, and Julie found herself completely absorbed in the task.

Chris leaned back on his haunches and watched her as she meticulously placed the covered bridge by the edge of the mirrored pond. There was no hint on her features of the agony she'd felt the night before, nor was there the taut control that usually kept her face emotionless.

Instead, there was a softness to her features that drew him, a tranquillity in her eyes that encouraged him. Yet he knew the tranquillity was momentary, a delicate state that she could lose at any moment.

He wanted to talk to her about what they had shared last night, the moment of desire that had flared so intensely, so unexpectedly between them. But he was afraid that by bringing it up, he would shatter the peace that, at the moment, kept her features relaxed and beautiful. So he contented himself to merely sit and look at her, tamping down the flames of desire that licked at his insides.

"There," she said, immense satisfaction glowing on her face as she placed the last ice-skating figurine on the mirrored surface of the pond. She sat back and viewed the community she had created.

"It's a wonderful village," he said, smiling at her, pleased when she returned the smile with one of her own.

"Yes, it is," she agreed. "And you've got the train all put together," she observed.

He nodded. "All it needs is the flick of a switch to set it in motion."

"Well?" She looked at him expectantly.

He laughed and stood up, holding out his hand to help her up. "You really have to stand back to get the full effect," he explained, pulling her up and reluctantly letting go of her hand.

With a dramatic flourish, he pushed the button. The train immediately responded by shining its lights and chugging around the tracks. As the locomotive approached the crossroads sign, its whistle resounded, and Julie clapped her hands together in delight. "Oh, Chris, it's wonderful!"

"Yes, it is," he said softly, wishing he could do something every moment of every day to keep the look of awe and happiness on her face.

"Get that thing away from me!" Mabel's strident voice rang out from the kitchen, followed by Doc's lower tones. "Chris! Chris, get in here and get this lunatic away from me."

Chris exchanged a look of puzzlement with Julie and together they went into the kitchen, where Doc had Mabel backed against the wall.

He held a sprig of mistletoe over her head.

"Get this fool away from me—he's done lost his mind," Mabel demanded.

"Don't be such an old grouch," Doc protested. "It's a harmless Christmas tradition to steal a kiss under the mistletoe."

"If you think I'm going to give you a kiss, then somebody's stolen your brain," Mabel retorted, waving her apron to punctuate her sentence.

With a disgruntled sigh, Doc moved away from her, pocketing the plastic sprig. "This house is filled with goodwill. I don't know why some of it doesn't seep into her mean bones," he said to Chris and Julie as he stomped out of the kitchen.

"Crazy old coot," Mabel exclaimed, straightening her apron, her cheeks flaming a vivid pink. She glared at Chris and Julie as if it was all their fault. "I'll kiss him, but I'll kiss him when I'm good and ready. Not because he's swinging some silly berries over my head." Cheeks still red with indignation, she, too, stomped out of the kitchen.

Julie stared wordlessly at Chris. As she saw the corner of his mouth quivering with suppressed laughter, she felt a bubble of merriment rising up inside her. She allowed its release, pleased to hear Chris's deep laughter mingling with her own, filling up every space of the kitchen.

It was one of those crazy moments, when laughter fed on laughter to produce more. Julie had no control. It was as if the giggles had been trapped inside her for too long and now positively refused to be stanched.

It felt good, and without thought she surrendered, allowing the alien emotion of mirth to shake her body, weaken her knees and blur her vision.

The little girl clapped her hands together in glee, letting the sounds of her momma's laughter roll over her, through her.

She loved it when her mother was happy. She wondered if her momma knew how pretty she looked when she laughed. How her eyes were warm and brown like a cup of hot cocoa, and the sound was like the bells her mother hung on the front door that tinkled every time anyone walked into their apartment.

She knew her momma had been sad since she'd gone away. If only there was some way to let her know that it was all right to laugh. She needed to let her know that it was okay to be happy without her.

Livvy drew her legs up beneath her, her forehead puckered in thought. There must be some way she could let her momma know that the only way Livvy could really be happy was if *she* was really happy.

She frowned, and rolled over on her tummy, her legs waving in the air behind her. Her tummy was her thinking side and this was going to take a lot of thought. This was definitely a problem...harder even than learning to write the letters to her name. There had to be something she could do...there just *had* to be.

Julie sat down at the desk in the small office off the great room, wondering if she'd lost her mind in offering to help Chris with his bookkeeping.

At the time it had seemed a reasonable thing to do. It would give her something to occupy her time while the house was overrun with children. Besides, it was a small way she could repay Chris for everything he had done for her.

But now, looking at the incredible mess of papers littering the desktop, she wondered if she hadn't gotten in over her head. "All we need here is a little organization," she muttered to herself, wading through the papers and making stacks of related receipts, bills and miscellaneous.

As she worked, she was vaguely conscious of the sounds of laughter coming from the great room, the noise of the kids who'd arrived on a bus an hour earlier. She smiled as she heard Chris's deep, convincing "ho ho ho," and listened to the kids' excited chattering.

She focused back on the work at hand, shaking her head ruefully as she saw how many of the bills were overdue. According to his ledger balance, the reason they had not been paid wasn't due to a lack of funds.

In fact, looking at the figures, Julie realized that in most circles Chris would be considered a wealthy man.

As the afternoon wore on and she continued to work, a portrait of Chris Kringle began to emerge. Julie had always believed if you wanted to really know somebody, all you had to do was study their checkbook. Most people showed their true personalities in their spending.

According to his records, Chris had his monetary finger in a variety of pies. Besides the North Pole, he owned a tree nursery in Denver and a thriving craft business that apparently sold the wooden villages he created. He was co-owner of a craft shop in Central City and a partner in a flower shop in the same tourist town. His books showed him to be a successful entrepreneur and he would have been obscenely wealthy if not for one thing: for every dollar he made, it appeared he gave a dollar away. There were irregular generous checks to a variety of charities, including a school for the blind in Denver, a reputable institution involved in research on childhood diseases and something called the School For Children.

Somehow, Julie wasn't surprised to learn of this dimension to Chris. He carried his charity and giving spirit in the warmth of his blue eyes, in the gentleness of his smile. He was a good man who'd found his joy in the act of giving.

She sighed, thinking how easy it would be to fall beneath the spell of Chris. He offered warmth to ease her cold, he met her darkness with an illuminating light. His kisses had promised a desire so intense, it would pull her out of her bubble of safe detachment from the world around her. She wasn't ready for that, wasn't sure she would ever be.

Consciously she willed herself to once again concentrate on the paperwork before her.

She was interrupted sometime later by a soft knock on the office door. Leaning back in the chair, she smiled as Chris stuck his head in. "You've been at it for hours. How about an eggnog break?" He held out a mug of the thick, rich drink.

"That looks wonderful," she agreed, standing up and reaching for the mug.

"Come on out here and relax. The kids left a few minutes ago and all is quiet for the moment."

She nodded, following him out of the office and into the great room, where they both sat down on the sofa. Julie sipped the eggnog and grinned at him. He hadn't changed from his Santa suit and his beard and mustache were still a snowy white.

"What?" he asked, his lips curved upward to return her smile. "What's so funny?"

"I've never had eggnog with Santa Claus before."

His grin widened. "Even Santa occasionally enjoys the finer things in life."

"Hmm, and eggnog is definitely one of the finer," Julie said, taking another sip. "I've got a stack of checks ready for you to sign." She looked at him curiously. "What's the School For Children? I couldn't help but notice that it seems to be a favorite charity of yours."

"It is," he agreed. "The school is five miles from here—a boarding school of sorts for kids who are having problems. They're the kids who are putting on the Christmas program."

"Problems? What sort of problems?" she asked, thinking in particular of the little boy who'd been so open and friendly with her.

"Different kinds. Adjustment problems, learning disabilities...most all of them just seem to need a lot of attention and a lot of love. The teachers and counselors at the school do what they can, but money is always tight for places like that.''

''And the kids are important to you.''

He nodded. ''The kids are the future.''

A shaft of pain incised Julie's heart. Yes, whenever she had looked into Livvy's eyes, she'd seen the hope of the future, the continuity of life, a progression of lineage . . . love.

''Julie?'' Chris's soft voice yanked her back from the dangerous precipice where she had momentarily teetered. She smiled at him gratefully and finished the eggnog.

''So, what's the story on Benjamin? Why is he at the school?''

Chris's smile held his obvious affection for the young boy. ''Benjamin was being raised by a single mother, a woman who's been battling alcoholism. A year ago, when she checked herself into a clinic for treatment, she placed Benjamin at the school. Since that time she's been in and out of hospitals, never really well enough to have him return home.''

''How sad,'' Julie observed.

''Benjamin will be all right. He's a survivor with a natural optimistic outlook.'' His smile widened. ''You definitely made a hit with him.''

''Me?'' She looked at him in surprise.

Chris nodded. "He said you have hair like an angel and smell like a flower. I think there's a crush of major proportion in the works."

"He seemed very sweet," she said, standing up from the sofa. "And now I think I'll go freshen up before supper."

He also stood, taking her mug from her.

"Thanks for the eggnog. Those checks are on the desk waiting for your signature," she said.

He nodded and set the two mugs down on the coffee table. "I just thought of something else I'll bet you've never done before," he said, and before she could guess his intent, he pulled her into his arms and placed his lips on hers.

The kiss lasted only a moment, just long enough for her to taste the lingering sweetness of eggnog, feel the tickling prickle of his white-stiffened mustache.

As he released her, she stepped back from him. He looked like a department-store Santa, but he kissed like Chris. It was slightly disconcerting, and more than a little wonderful.

"You shouldn't do that," she admonished, knowing her voice held no conviction whatsoever.

He grinned, a sexy one that was instantly at odds with his costume. "I told you Santa occasionally enjoyed the finer things in life. And kissing you, Julie, is definitely one of them."

"I think you've been cooped up here with your reindeer too long," she returned, trying to keep the mood light and easy even though her lips still tingled from the brief contact with his.

He reached out and gently touched the side of her face. "No, I just like kissing you," he answered softly. He dropped his hand and laughed, easing the tension that suddenly sang through Julie. "Surely you won't make me resort to sneak attacks with mistletoe—like Doc?"

She shook her head and smiled. "But it's very disconcerting to kiss the man I used to beg to bring me a baby doll that wets its diapers and drinks from a bottle."

He laughed again, his gaze warm... so warm as it lingered on her face. "And what is it you want Santa to bring you for Christmas this year?" he asked.

Livvy. The wish trembled on her lips, filled her brain with want, with need. *Bring me back my baby.* But she knew that was impossible.

She looked sadly at Chris. He was such a good man and she knew he genuinely wanted to make her Christmas wish come true. But even Santa Claus with his magic red bag couldn't pull off a miracle.

"You can't give me what I want for Christmas... nobody can." This time it was she who reached up and touched the side of his face, her fingers lingering on the warmth of his skin. "But thank you for caring," she murmured. She turned and started up the stairs, then turned back and looked at him.

From the distance, he looked every inch the part of the man he played. In his red, fur-trimmed suit and shiny black boots, he looked as if he'd just stepped off the front of a holiday greeting card.

As Santa Claus, he could offer her candy canes and eggnog, twinkling eyes and merriment. As Chris, he could give her drugging kisses and addictive caresses. He could offer her moments of relief from her inner pain—but they were just brief moments, and always the grief returned, more potent than ever.

She turned and continued up the stairs, her thoughts still filled with the man in the Santa suit. He was a good man, and he deserved a woman who could care about him with an intensity to match his own. He deserved a woman who would embrace life with the same energy he did. She knew with a certainty she would never, could never be that woman. Her love, her life had been buried with Livvy. Julie was dead inside, and it was only a matter of time before Chris realized it.

Chapter Seven

Julie saw Livvy standing across the street with her schoolmates. Her white fur coat blended in with the snow covering the school grounds.

Julie smiled, returning Livvy's excited wave. The child's cherub face radiated her intense excitement. Julie could tell by the way Livvy danced from foot to foot that she was impatient for the school crossing guard to let her run across the street, so that the afternoon of shopping for last-minute Christmas presents could begin.

Julie had promised her daughter all week that today they would shop, eat at their favorite pizza place, then visit Santa Claus for one last plea for a puppy.

A grin touched Julie's lips as she thought of the cocker spaniel puppy that would be delivered to her doorstep first thing Christmas morning, complete with a big red bow tied around his neck. Livvy would be beside herself. She'd wanted a puppy for so long, and finally Julie had agreed.

With an impatient sigh of her own, Julie wrapped her coat more tightly around her, wishing she'd remembered her gloves. It smelled like snow, and the forecasters were predicting another two inches before Christmas. She turned her attention back to the schoolchildren.

Suddenly Julie knew she was dreaming. She knew it, because as the crossing guard walked out into the center of the intersection and held up her bright red Stop sign, everything began to move in slow motion.

She knew with a dreadful certainty what was going to happen. She'd witnessed it over and over again in her dreams, been tortured by the same vision countless times.

"No..." She struggled to wake up, knowing where the dream would take her, where it would end. She was afraid she would go mad if she had to watch it another time. "No!"

But the scene played out. As the crossing guard raised her arm and signaled for the children to begin their walk across the street, instead of trying to wake up, Julie tried to change fate. "Livvy, no! Stay there, baby. Don't cross the street!"

However, it was like they were players on two separate planes of reality, Julie trapped in the present, and Livvy merely a specter from the past. The little girl couldn't hear her mother's desperate pleas. She waved gaily one more time, then ran out into the street.

The car came from nowhere. Too fast, dangerously fast. The driver apparently didn't see the crossing guard until the very last minute. He swerved to miss her, and hit the little girl in the furry white coat, sending her careening through the air like a soft, pliable snowball.

For a long moment there was an eerie, unearthly kind of silence. Not a child on the curb made a sound. The car had instantly been shut off with the impact.

Suddenly Julie heard screaming...a loud keening noise that rose and fell like the chilled wind that blew through her. With a start, she realized the noise was coming from herself. And it continued as she made her way to where Livvy lay so still....

"Julie...Julie."

She fought against the restraining arms, needing to go to her child, wanting to somehow breathe life back into the little body.

"Julie...wake up. You're having a nightmare."

She struggled with the words, trying to find a place where they made sense in her mind. With an effort she opened her eyes and looked into the deep blue ones of Chris.

"Chris?" She reached up to touch his face, to assure herself of place and time. Then the horror of what she'd just relived returned. With a choked sob, his face blurred beneath a mist of tears.

"Shhh, it's all right." He gathered her into his arms, holding her against the strength and warmth of his bare chest. He rocked her gently back and forth, stroking her hair and murmuring soft words of comfort like a parent soothing the troubled sleep of a child.

Within minutes, Julie's tears had ceased, leaving behind a black ache of emptiness she'd grown accustomed to, a black ache that threatened to engulf her entirely.

She finally pushed away from Chris, suddenly too aware of the bareness of his chest, too conscious of her own silky nightgown that barely made a stab at modesty. "I'm sorry... I'm all right now."

Chris released her, but didn't get up from the edge of the bed where he sat. "It must have been some nightmare," he observed.

"Worse than a nightmare...it was a memory." She shivered beneath the weight of the dream, wondering how many more times she would have to relive that horrible moment that had destroyed her life.

"Tell me about it," he urged, his eyes oceans of compassion. She shook her head, unwilling to share the grief of the death of a child he didn't even know.

She'd seen the way the loss of a child affected people. When Livvy had first died, she'd tried to talk about her to everyone, anyone who would listen. She'd needed to talk about her, but it made others uncomfortable. "Don't dwell on it," her friends had said, averting their eyes from the pain in hers. "Put it behind you," they'd suggested, tactfully changing the subject.

Julie had learned early and well to hug her grief, her memories, and the essence of Livvy close to her heart, mourning in solitude, anguishing alone.

"Julie, please talk to me. I need to know. I need to understand." He picked up one of her hands, tracing the lines in her palm like a fortune-teller attempting to predict the future, analyze the past. "Julie, help me understand." His voice trembled with his need, and she realized she couldn't deny him. He'd been too kind. He'd somehow come too close.

She sighed, moving out of the bed and reaching for her robe, needing its warmth wrapped around her, needing to pace as she relived the horror of losing Livvy. Chris remained on the bed, watching her expectantly.

"The dream was the memory of the day my daughter died." Before he could comment, say any inane words of sorrow, she went on, telling him of the accident that had stolen Livvy away from her. The words came out of her tightly controlled, almost emotionless as she explained the way it had happened. "She was hit by a car as she crossed the street after school. The driver was drunk," she explained. "High on holiday spirit and rum punch from an office party."

"What happened to him?"

Julie shrugged. "I don't know. The first couple of months after the accident went by in a haze for me." She moved to the window and stared out into the darkness of the night, a darkness that mirrored the one inside her heart. "Olivia was my life. My husband walked out on me when I was four months pregnant, so from the very beginning it was just Livvy and me."

The control she'd held on to so tightly, the emotions she'd kept under such rein, gave way and she turned back to look at Chris, a veil of tears shimmering her vision. She held her arms out before her, arms heavy with emptiness. "I wake up in the night and my arms ache to hold her. I don't know how to live without her," she finally whispered.

Chris left the bed and came to stand next to her, but he didn't touch her, knew she was at a place where his touch would push her over the edge. "Tell me about her, Julie. You've told me about her death. Now tell me about her life."

She looked at him sharply, her lips trembling uncontrollably. Gently he led her back over to the bed, where they both sat down once again. "Tell me about your Livvy," he said softly. And she did.

She told him of the night Livvy was born, of the moment when the doctor had placed the baby in her arms. Julie had held Livvy close, smelling her sweet scent, running her finger across the downy scalp, and she'd believed in miracles. "She never walked when she could run, never spoke when she could sing. She embraced life with both hands and squeezed it for all it was worth."

The stories fell out of Julie, one right after the other, painting a vivid picture for Chris to see, a picture of a special little girl who'd brought joy to everyone around her.

As Julie spoke, the tension ebbed out of her and her brown eyes softened and her smile grew achingly lovely. Chris wanted to absorb her pain, make it disappear forever, but he knew it would always be a part of her. Livvy would always be a part of her.

He now understood so much—her detachment from the world around her, her sudden bouts of anguish. He wished he knew what he could do to make it easier for her to live with the tragedy of losing her child.

As she continued to reminisce, he put an arm around her shoulders and she nestled in beside him. They remained that way long into the night, Julie talking of Livvy and Chris merely listening.

It wasn't until she had paused for a few minutes...minutes that stretched longer and longer, that he realized she had fallen asleep. He merely tightened his embrace around her, drinking in her heady fragrance, satisfied that her features were relaxed and unstressed in slumber. He had a feeling there would be no more bad dreams, at least not for the remainder of the night.

She had purged herself by talking of her pain, released her grief and replaced it with happy memories.

Reluctantly, he lay her down and covered her up with the blankets. She didn't stir. She slept deeply, soundly, her breaths barely moving her chest.

He reached out a hand and gently stroked a strand of her shining golden hair, wishing he could erase all the pain that had marred her life to this point. To lose a child had to be the greatest adversity a parent would ever face, and as he thought of the anguish Julie suffered, he felt a tightening in his own chest, an uncomfortable fullness in his heart.

But a greater tragedy would be if Julie gave up on life, if she grew bitter and refused to accept love back into her heart.

It would take a miracle, but somehow Chris had to convince Julie that she had to continue to live life to its fullest. She needed to know that it was okay to be happy, that Livvy would always have a place in her memories, and would always be an angel in her pocket in the future. But thoughts of the little girl shouldn't be a deterrent to Julie's future.

Yes, it would take a miracle, but that didn't daunt Chris. After all, Santa Claus dealt in miracles every day.

Leaning over, he gently kissed Julie's temple, then went back to his own room.

She awoke feeling good. It surprised her, the well-being that greeted her when she opened her eyes.

She'd grown so accustomed to awakening with the heavy dread of facing another day alone.

As she showered, she thought about the middle-of-the-night conversation she'd shared with Chris. Oh, how good it had been to share memories of Livvy instead of mentally shoving them aside. How wonderful it had been to wallow in the past, enjoy her baby vicariously by telling a stranger about her.

Dressed, she looked at her reflection, pleased to see that her bruise had faded to the point where makeup covered the last of the discoloration. At least it would be all healed by the time she got back to her job in Denver.

She smiled as she thought of what she would tell Kathy about why she hadn't stayed at the cabin. Would Kathy believe her when Julie told her she'd spent the holidays with Chris Kringle? Probably not . . . Julie wasn't quite sure she believed it herself.

Her smile slowly faded as she thought of leaving here. Strange how suddenly this place felt comfortable. After last night, there were no more secrets in her heart. Chris knew her pain, had shared it with her. More importantly, he'd let her tell him about every special moment, every wonderful thing Livvy had ever said or done.

Julie was surprised to realize it would be difficult to say goodbye to these people who had been so kind to her, people who had managed to secure a special place in her heart.

She turned away from the mirror and headed downstairs to the kitchen, where Mabel was already dressed in her long red skirt, white blouse and green apron... her costume whenever they were expecting guests.

"Good morning." Julie greeted the older woman cheerfully. "Buses coming early this morning?"

"Any minute," Mabel said. "There won't be any rest for any of us between now and Christmas morning. The last couple days before Christmas Day are always hectic as can be."

"Is there anything I can do to help?" Julie asked.

Mabel smiled at her gratefully. "How about you make a fresh pot of coffee? Doc should be in any minute from feeding the animals, and he always likes his coffee fresh."

Julie nodded and busied herself with the coffeemaker. "It looks like it's going to be a gorgeous day," she observed, noticing the early-morning sunshine glistening on the snow.

"The weatherman says it's supposed to get near forty-five degrees." Mabel shook her head. "That means slush and mud all over my floors."

"I'll help you clean them up this evening," Julie offered.

"Bless you, honey, but I'm used to cleaning floors. I just like to hear the sound of my own voice grumbling."

"That's the truest thing I've ever heard fall out of your mouth," Doc said as he entered the kitchen. "But I still think you're the most gorgeous woman I've ever known."

"Oh, how you do blather," Mabel retorted, her cheeks flaming brightly.

Julie watched this exchange with amusement, realizing their banter was actually a form of flirtation that they both enjoyed.

"What would you like for breakfast?" Mabel asked Doc as Julie poured the water into the machine, standing back as it steamed and gurgled.

"I'd like a plate of pancakes and a big fat kiss." Doc reared back in his chair and winked at Julie.

"You want the syrup in your lap?" Mabel asked.

"No," Doc answered.

"Then I suppose you'll just have pancakes."

"I suppose you're right," he agreed grudgingly, then grinned at Julie. "She's a hard woman, Julie. I think she takes pleasure in breaking my heart."

"I'd take more pleasure in breaking your head," Mabel retorted, causing both Doc and Julie to laugh.

"Ah, that's what a man likes to hear first thing in the morning," Chris said as he entered the kitchen.

He was clad in his Santa Claus suit and his gaze was warm on Julie. "Did you sleep well?" he asked.

She nodded. "Better than I have in months." She smiled at him, their nighttime conversation yielding a strange sort of intimacy between them. "Thank you," she said softly.

He tipped an imaginary hat. "Anytime I can be of service."

"Did I miss something here?" Mabel asked, looking curiously at them both.

"Nothing we're going to discuss," Chris answered, laughing as Julie's cheeks blushed hotly.

Mabel eyed Julie, then Chris, suspiciously. Then, with a knowing grunt, she turned back to the stove.

They had all barely finished breakfast when the first bus lumbered through the gates, the sounds of the children audible despite the distance. "Oh, dear, I knew I should have had breakfast ready earlier," Mabel exclaimed, eyeing the dirty dishes in dismay.

"You go on and greet the kids. I'll take care of the dishes," Julie said, shooing away Mabel's protests. As the three left to attend to the guests, Julie cleared off the table and loaded the dishwasher.

When the kitchen was spotless, she turned to leave, but paused at the window, spotting Chris who stood in the middle of the yard surrounded by dozens of kids.

She smiled, realizing that even the thick padding around his waist and the fur-lined suit couldn't completely camouflage his attractiveness. The broadness of his shoulders was evident, as was the slimness of his hips. She knew if she opened the window, she would be able to hear his deep laughter. The thought sent a sudden shiver up her spine ... a delicious shiver of pleasure. He was definitely the sexiest Santa she'd ever seen.

With a small shake of her head, uncomfortable with the direction her thoughts were taking, she turned away from the window and headed for the little office off the great room. If she worked real hard for the day, then she should be able to get Chris's books completely organized. That was the least she could do.

Chris answered the phone on the second ring, flopping tiredly into a chair at the kitchen table. "Hi, Charley," he greeted the mechanic, waving at Mabel as she entered the kitchen.

"Sure, I'll give her a message." He listened, frowning as he realized what the message was. "First thing in the morning? That was really fast." He shot a quick glance at Mabel, who was busy unloading the dishwasher. "Uh ... look, Charley, could you hold off for a couple more days, at least until Christmas? Yeah, that's right. Thanks. We'll see you then."

He slowly hung up the receiver, refusing to look at Mabel, who had stopped her chore and now stood glaring at him. "Whew, what a day," he said, standing up and finally looking at her in innocence. "I guess I'll just head upstairs and get out of this suit. I'm really beat."

"Hmm . . . manipulation always wears one out," Mabel observed.

He grimaced sheepishly. "Okay, so I manipulated a little. Charley has Julie's car ready, but I think it would be best if she stayed here until after Christmas. Her daughter was killed on the day before Christmas Eve," he reminded Mabel, having already discussed the matter with her earlier in the day. "She shouldn't be alone in some isolated cabin. Yes, I'm manipulating, but don't you see it's for the best?"

"Oh, I see, all right," Mabel said, looking at him assessingly. "I see that you're falling in love with that woman."

Chris stared at her incredulously. "That's the most ridiculous thing I've ever heard," he uttered. "I just want to help her through a rough time, that's all. I . . . I want to help her heal, and I think if she can get through this first anniversary, she'll be all right," he finished.

"And what happens when she's all healed up?" Mabel asked.

"Then she leaves here and goes on to lead a full, happy life," Chris answered. But as the words left his lips, he felt a curious sort of sorrow of his own.

Chapter Eight

"Julie, hand me a red one," Chris yelled down from his perch on top of the ladder.

Julie dug through the box of colored light bulbs and handed him the crimson one he'd requested. She tilted her head back and watched as he removed the burned-out bulb and replaced the new one in the string of lights that hung above the front door of the house.

"I think that does it," he said, descending the ladder to stand next to her. He plugged the strand back into the outside outlet, smiling in satisfaction as each individual bulb lit up. "I also noticed several burned-out ones on the wreath at the side of the house," he said, picking up the ladder and carrying it around the corner.

Julie followed after him with the box of new bulbs, enjoying the feel of the afternoon sunshine through the back of her coat. The weather had been unusually mild for the past two days and Chris had spent most of his free time readying the outside of the house for the guests who would arrive the following night for the Christmas program.

Julie had spent the past two days getting Chris's books in order and helping Mabel bake special goodies to be served after the program. They had been pleasant days filled with activity and laughter.

The only uncomfortable moments had come when she'd found herself alone with Chris. She enjoyed his company, liked the way his laughter came so easily, the way he stroked his beard with his thumb and forefinger when in deep thought. But there was an inexplicable simmering energy between them that made her distinctly uncomfortable.

She now looked up at him, admiring the way his dark hair shone in the sunshine, the way his heavy flannel shirt stretched taut across his broad back as he reached to grab the strand of lights. She flushed and averted her gaze.

Who was she fooling? She knew exactly what the energy was that throbbed in the air between them whenever they were alone. It was desire, pure and simple. The truth of the matter was there was a part of her that wanted to do wonderfully sinful things with Santa Claus.

She shoved these thoughts from her mind. How could she even think such things? How could she even entertain the idea of making love to a man, of finding happiness in a strong embrace?

It had been a year ago today that her happiness had been forever stolen from her. Exactly a year ago today. She shivered, the sun overhead seeming to lose its warmth.

"I need two blues and a red," Chris called to her, pulling her from her introspection.

She nodded, eager to place her thoughts on the task at hand. It took him only a moment to replace the faulty lights and climb back down the ladder. "That should do it," he said. "I think we're all set for tomorrow night."

"Are the kids ready for the program?" Julie asked, following him as he carried the ladder to the barn.

"We'll know tonight at dress rehearsal."

"How many people are you expecting to show up to watch the big event?"

He leaned the ladder against a wall, then turned back to her with a shrug of his shoulders. "I'm never sure how many to expect. We seldom get many of the kids' parents, but most of the teachers from the school and their families show up. We also get a lot of the neighboring families who come to show their support.'' He gestured for her to precede him out of the barn. ''I figure we'll probably get between twenty and thirty people if the good weather holds.''

As they walked across the melting snow, he casually placed an arm around her shoulder. *It's just a gesture of friendship,* she told herself. Yet the weight of it, the feel of its masculine strength around her, reminded her of things she'd forgotten. Like the joy and wonder of being in love, sharing hopes and dreams with a special man, the awe of giving herself completely to another.

She grimaced, realizing these weren't forgotten pleasures—they were merely ones she'd determined she would never have again. Livvy would never again dance in the snow. She would never laugh again. She was in a cold and dark place. Was she afraid? Lonely? It was these thoughts, these fears, that would always and forever keep Julie from reaching out for happiness again.

She now looked up at Chris. ''Why aren't you married?'' she asked, suddenly wondering why a man like him hadn't committed himself to a woman, as he had apparently committed himself to this place and the children in the area.

He shrugged, removing his arm from around her and instead grabbing her elbow to help her across a slippery patch of ice. "I almost got married years ago. Thankfully, before we could actually tie the knot, we discovered we both wanted very different things in life. I told her about my ideas for this place, and she thought I was completely crazy."

"And now?" Julie asked.

He released her elbow and grinned at her. "Now everyone knows I'm crazy." He sobered slightly, his gaze lingering on her. "I guess I have yet to find the woman who can share my life. It will take a very special woman to be Mrs. Chris Kringle."

He opened the back door for her. They walked into the kitchen and into the middle of a major commotion. Doc stood on a chair and worked a plunger up and down in the kitchen sink.

Mabel stood next to him, wringing her apron. She turned worried eyes to Chris and Julie. "The sink is plugged up," she explained. "I don't know how I'm going to fix dinner or do dishes or anything."

"I told you I'll fix it and I will," Doc exclaimed, pausing in his plunging to swipe his perspiring forehead.

"Maybe we should just call a plumber," Mabel said, worrying her apron into a twisted piece of fabric.

"There's no need," Doc protested. "I said I'll fix it." He began to work the plunger up and down once again, his face growing red with his efforts.

"Is there anything I can do to help?" Chris asked.

"Nope," Doc answered, his chest puffing. "I may be old, but a stuffed sink isn't going to get the best of me...no way." The sink gurgled as it unclogged, and Doc grinned triumphantly.

"Bend down here," Mabel demanded, looking up at the red-faced, puffing old man.

He swiped his forehead with the back of her hand and looked at her impatiently. "What?"

"I want you to bend down," Mabel repeated. She smiled coyly. "I want to give you a kiss."

"Now?" Doc looked at her incredulously.

"Well, if you don't want me to..." Mabel allowed her words to trail off, a miffed expression on her face.

Doc quickly bent over, allowing her to capture his face between her hands. With a girlish giggle, Mabel planted a smacking kiss on his cheek. She then stepped back and smiled at Chris and Julie in satisfaction. "I told you I'd kiss him when I was good and ready, and not a minute before."

Doc straightened up, his gaze going up to the heavens. "Please, please, before I die, let me understand the way a woman's mind works," he said.

"Ah, Doc, I'm afraid that's one of the last mysteries left of life," Chris said with a laugh. He touched Julie on the shoulder and motioned for her to follow him out of the room.

"They're quite a pair," Julie said with a small smile as they entered the great room.

"That's a romance that has been interesting to watch." He sat down on the sofa. "They're good for each other. They both need somebody to aggravate, torment . . . and love."

Julie laughed, gently touching one of the ornaments on the Christmas tree. "They definitely give new meaning to the rules of courtship."

Chris moved off the sofa and came to stand next to her. "Everyone needs somebody special in their life," he said, his breath a warm fan against the side of her face.

"Or the memory of somebody special," Julie replied.

Chris's gaze penetrated her, as if he was trying to look someplace deep inside her, find a hidden piece of her heart. "Are memories enough?" he asked softly.

She hesitated a moment. "They have to be." She touched the ornament one last time, then moved away from him, uncomfortable with his closeness, filled with a sudden restless energy. "If you'll excuse me, I think I'll go on upstairs. I've got some things I want to do before dinner."

Moments later, in the solitude of her room, she paced the floor back and forth, thinking of Mabel and Doc, thinking about Livvy and, finally, thinking about Chris. Somehow, things were getting all jumbled up in her head. Nothing was quite as clear-cut as it had been. Even her grief seemed different somehow.

"No." The denial escaped her on a sigh. Nothing had changed. Livvy was still gone and Julie hugged her grief to her as a testimony to the love she'd felt for her child. She felt somehow that to let go of any of the grief was to disavow the love she felt for Livvy.

The restless energy continued to plague her for the remainder of the day. She picked at her dinner, mentally isolating herself from the conversation of the other three.

Later that evening, she stood at the window of her room, looking out into the darkness. A year ago today her life had been destroyed. Memories shot through her—happy ones, tragic ones. Her grief was back full-fledged, filling her up with the kind of black despair that had recently been a familiar companion.

She welcomed it. This, at least, was not confusing, but was clean and clear-cut, unlike so many of the emotions that had assailed her the past couple of days.

She sighed, wrapping her arms around herself and staring out at the bleak blackness of night. Livvy was forever in the blackness. She would never again feel the warmth of the sun on her face. She would never again hear the birds singing in the trees.

Julie leaned her forehead against the cold windowpane, surprised to realize that the grief wasn't as welcome as she'd initially thought. She preferred the safe numbness that she'd felt before arriving at the North Pole.

Now, for the first time, it was too much—the grief was no longer welcome, but overwhelming. Julie wanted an escape from her own thoughts and emotions. She needed to be where there was life... laughter.

Without giving herself a chance to change her mind, she headed downstairs, where she put on a coat and boots and stepped out the back door. The snow that had melted in the warmth of the day, had refrozen and created a crusty topping that crunched under her feet.

She walked toward the shed, knowing the activity there would fill her thoughts, make it impossible for her to dwell in her past.

"I won't wear it . . . it's a dress." Julie heard Benjamin's voice as she walked through the door. She slid into a seat and watched as Chris tried to handle the disgruntled child.

"It's what the wise men wore," Chris stressed, gesturing at the other two boys, who both were dressed in costumes. "The others are wearing them."

Benjamin crossed his arms over his chest and shook his head. "Boys don't wear dresses," he exclaimed succinctly.

Julie saw Chris's frustration and on impulse she got up and approached the stage. "Hi," she said, smiling at Benjamin.

"Hi," Chris returned, flashing her a tight smile.

"What's going on?" she asked.

Chris expelled a weary sigh. "Benjamin won't wear his costume. He says wise men don't wear dresses."

"He's absolutely right," Julie agreed, seeing Chris's distraught reaction. "Wise men don't wear dresses, they wear robes." She took the costume from Chris's hands and held it up. "And this is a beautiful robe."

Benjamin uncrossed his arms and looked at her uncertainly. "A robe?"

Julie nodded and helped him slip it on. She tied the sash around his chubby tummy and stepped back, eyeing him critically. "Wonderful. Now you look dignified and handsome and especially wise."

Benjamin straightened his shoulders and a smile curved his lips. "Okay, I'll wear it," he agreed.

"Great. Let's get on with the rehearsal," Chris said, flashing Julie a grateful smile.

As the rehearsal continued, Julie slipped back to her seat, watching as the kids performed their parts and sang their songs. She closed her eyes, envisioning Livvy on stage, wearing one of the simple costumes, her eyes shining with excitement, her voice rising above the others as she sang. The sounds of the play rehearsal faded as the vision intensified.

"Are you sleeping?"

Julie frowned, recognizing Benjamin's voice, smelling the little-boy scent that emanated from him. Reluctantly she opened her eyes, watching as Benjamin slid into the seat next to her. "No, I'm not sleeping," she answered softly, realizing that Chris must have called for a break. The kids were gathered around him, and he was serving cookies and punch.

"You want some punch?" Benjamin asked. "I could go get you some."

Julie shook her head, wanting only to drift back into the world of her visions, the pleasure of her memories. "Why don't you run along and join your friends?" she said not unkindly.

He smiled shyly. "I don't want to. I like sitting here with you." His feet began their rhythmic swing and he looked at her curiously. "Are you married?" he asked.

"No, I'm divorced."

"So's my mom," he replied. "Do you have any kids?"

Julie's heart tightened. "Yes, I...I have a little girl."

Benjamin's smile widened. "Where is she?"

"I... She died last year in a car accident."

"So she's in heaven."

"I suppose," she answered, her hands convulsively grasping the fabric of her coat. She wanted Benjamin to go away. She wanted this conversation immediately ended. "I think you'd better get back onstage. They'll be starting the rehearsal again soon."

Benjamin ignored her attempt to send him on his way. "If your little girl is in heaven, then why do you look so sad? In heaven everything is pretty and nobody ever gets sick." He looked at Julie thoughtfully. "If I go to heaven before my mommy, I don't want her to be sad for me. Heaven is—"

"Benjamin, go back to the stage," Julie demanded, her pain overriding any other emotion.

"It's all right. I can stay here," he answered, oblivious to her anguish. "What was your little girl's name?"

Julie stood up, her body trembling. "I don't want to talk about this anymore." She was vaguely aware that she sounded angry, but she couldn't help it. Her torment now blinded her to everything around her. She only knew she had to stop the conversation, get away from the little boy with his bright eyes and childish scent. "Go back with the others, Benjamin."

"But I just—"

"Get out of here," she finally lashed out, instantly contrite as she saw the tears glistening in his eyes, his bottom lip quivering ominously. Before she could apologize to the little boy, Chris was at her side. He grabbed her elbow and firmly led her to the back of the shed.

When they were away from the children, he turned and glared at her, his eyes not the warm blue she had come to expect, but rather a chilling, arctic stare.

"What in the hell do you think you're doing?" he demanded in a harsh whisper.

"I..."

"How dare you come in here and vent your grief on a little boy? What gives you the right to snap at Benjamin and make him cry?" Chris's features were taut with anger, the grip on her elbow almost painful. "Livvy would be appalled at your behavior."

Julie stiffened and yanked her elbow out of his grip, responding with an anger of her own. "How dare you presume to know anything about my daughter and what she would think or feel?" she retorted, her emotions coiled in a tight ball in her chest, a ball that made her feel as if she were being strangled. "You have no right to talk about her. Besides, this is all your fault." She wrapped her arms around her stomach, sick with pain. "You should have taken me to a motel...you should have left me alone...you should have left me in my car to die," she finished with a desperate whisper.

He stared at her, his anger usurped by a look of disappointment, an overwhelming sadness. "Julie, Livvy is gone. We can't always know the reasons why people are taken from us, but we have to go on. If she's in heaven, it's because it was time for her to go. Now it's time for you to let go. You told me how

Livvy embraced life, how she loved to laugh. She would want you to go on."

"I don't know how." Then, not wanting to hear anymore, she wrapped her grief around her like an insulating shawl and ran out of the shed.

She ran as if trying to escape the heartache that now bit and gnawed at her insides like the vicious teeth of a wild animal.

She ran until she couldn't run any longer, until the cold night air burned her lungs and she collapsed into a snowdrift.

The silence of the night was complete, broken only by her gasps for breath and half-choked sobs.

Oh, Livvy, sweet Livvy. Her heart ached with the desire to cuddle Livvy against her, smell the sunshine fragrance of her hair. It wasn't supposed to be this way. Children weren't supposed to die before their parents.

She rolled over on her back, staring up at the millions of stars overhead. Which one was Livvy? Julie's mother had once told her that the stars were angels winking.

Julie squeezed her eyes tightly closed as icy tears oozed down her cheeks. No, children weren't supposed to die before their parents. That wasn't the natural order of things.

Without consciously evoking it, a vision of her own mother filled her mind. Her mother had passed away three years ago after an extended illness.

Julie could still remember the sharp, antiseptic scent of the hospital room, the soft, rhythmic bleeping of the heart monitor, the sound of her mother's labored breathing.

"Julie," her mother had uttered. She'd reached up and stroked Julie's cheek with one hand, the other reaching out to grip Julie's hand.

"I'm right here," Julie had replied.

Her mother had gazed at her, a loving smile on her lips as she swiped at Julie's tears. "Don't cry for me, Julie girl."

Julie had merely squeezed her mother's hand more tightly, unable to speak. "And don't be afraid for me," her mother had continued. "I'll be just fine as long as I know you're happy."

Chris's words now played and replayed in her mind. Was he right? Did Livvy want...*need* her happiness?

There was no doubt in Julie's mind that Livvy was in heaven, held in loving arms. There was also no doubt in her mind that a time would come when she would once again hold Livvy in her loving arms. But in the meantime, Julie had to choose how she was going to exist without Livvy.

She sat up, wiping away the tears from her raw, burning cheeks. Chris was right. Livvy had loved life, had especially loved Christmas. By turning her back on what her daughter had so loved, was Julie rejecting a part of Livvy herself?

Slowly, thoughtfully, Julie struggled to stand up, her gaze once again seeking the starlit skies. Millions of stars twinkled their brilliance. Some, Julie knew, had already burned themselves out and only their memory remained. Like Livvy, she thought. Her life light was gone, but the memory of that brilliance would linger through the years.

Yes, Livvy would want her to love, to laugh, to be filled with the spirit of Christmas. Releasing her grief didn't mean she had to release memories of her love for her daughter. She needed to live for Livvy. She needed to feel the sunshine that Livvy never again would; she wanted to embrace all of life in Livvy's honor.

Thinking about the tears that had spilled from Benjamin's eyes, shame welled up inside her. Chris was right—Livvy would have been appalled at Julie's self-absorbed behavior.

She owed a special little boy a great big apology. She owed Chris one, as well.

With this in mind, Julie walked back to the shed. She eased the door open and stood just inside.

The kids were reenacting the nativity. Baby Jesus was a doll in a cardboard box. Mary had bright red pigtails and cookie crumbs on her face. Joseph scratched under his arm with the unselfconsciousness of his age. A goat was eating the shepherd's staff and the angel's aluminum foil halo kept falling off her head.

It was a scene of precious chaos, and in the middle of it all was Chris, slapping the goat, fixing the halo and doing what he did best . . . offering loving encouragement to each and every child.

As their voices rose in unison to sing "Silent Night," tears once again trekked down Julie's cheeks. However these tears were different. As the childish voices filled the shed, and the words to the song flowed over her, Julie realized the tears that fell were cleansing, healing.

As they began to sing the song for a second time, Julie chimed in, singing as much with her heart as with her mouth, feeling the peace of acceptance slowly sweeping through her.

Livvy wrapped her arms around herself, listening to her mother's voice. She lay down, wrapping the sound around her like a warm, comforting blanket.

With a soft sigh of contentment, the little angel fell asleep with her mother's voice providing her bedtime lullaby.

Chapter Nine

"Would you mind if I rode with you to take the kids home?" Julie asked Chris when the rehearsal was finished for the night.

He looked at her in surprise. He'd seen her come back into the shed earlier, had seen her only moments before talking to Benjamin, obviously apologizing for the scene earlier. "You're welcome to ride along," he agreed.

Minutes later they were all loaded up in the sleigh, Julie and Chris up front, and the kids all behind them. The sleigh bells tinkled merrily, adding to the children's laughter and the cloppity-clop of the horses' hooves. The moon overhead was bright enough to illuminate the wintry landscape and paint it in silvery hues.

Chris looked over at Julie, noting how the moon-light sought the curves and hollows of her face, highlighted her hair with an ethereal glow. She must have felt his gaze on her, for she turned and looked at him, smiling hesitantly.

The smile eased Chris's concern. He'd been afraid he'd been too rough on her, overstepped himself with his words. Her smile somehow reassured him, made him want to reach out and stroke her cheek, taste her upturned lips.

He shook the reins, urging the horses a little faster, uncomfortable with the direction of his thoughts. He had a sleigh full of children. Now wasn't the time to be entertaining the idea of very un-Santa-like urges.

It took almost a half an hour to travel the distance to the school. Talk between the two adults was almost impossible as the children filled the night hush with singing and laughter. It wasn't until they had unloaded the kids and they were on their way home that Julie broke the silence between them.

"You were right, you know," she said softly as she pulled her coat collar more firmly around her neck.

"Right?" He looked at her curiously.

"The things you said to me, about Livvy wanting me to go on, wanting me to be happy."

He shrugged his shoulders, reining the horses to a sedate walk. "It's what I believe."

"And it's what I want to believe. I *need* to believe she's someplace up there looking down on me." She smiled up at him. "For the first time in a year, the possibility of life going on isn't quite so painful, and I néed to thank you for that."

"Don't thank me," he protested. "You're a strong woman, Julie. I've seen your strength in your eyes. Eventually you would have been all right without me." This time he didn't fight his impulse, but followed through on it. He placed his arm around her shoulders, pleased when she didn't stiffen, but rather, melted against the warmth of his side.

"Even though I know I have to go forward without Livvy, it still hurts."

He tightened his grip on her shoulder. "The hurt will never completely go away. Livvy will always have a place in your memory, a room in your heart. There will always be a bittersweet ache when you think of her face, when you mention her name. But you will learn to live with it. And you'll learn to celebrate life in her memory."

She looked up at him once again, her brown eyes sparkling with diamondlike tears. "How did you get to be such a wise man, Chris Kringle?'' she asked softly.

"Oh, I don't know—just lucky, I guess," he answered lightly.

She sighed, obviously exhausted by the past several hours of turmoil. As she leaned her head against his shoulder, Chris realized that sometime during the past couple of days, he'd fallen in love with her.

She'd be leaving here in the next day or two, going back to Denver to get on with her life. Her heart had begun to open and Chris knew she would be all right. He also knew that for a wise man he'd done an incredibly stupid thing of falling so helplessly in love with her. And it was time to let her go.

The morning of the pageant dawned cloudy and gray with the threat of snow heavy in the air. But a little thing like the weather couldn't daunt the high spirits of everyone.

"It won't snow until after the program," Chris exclaimed with the assurance of a man who'd had a personal conversation with the great weather maker in the sky.

Julie grinned at him, somehow believing that if he said it wouldn't snow . . . it wouldn't.

They'd spent most of the morning putting the finishing decorating touches in the shed. Evergreen boughs and holly sprigs had been attached to the ends of each bench. Red tablecloths had been placed on the tables that would later hold eggnog, punch and an assortment of cookies and sweets for the guests. The stage was readied, the props in place.

The afternoon had passed with Julie helping Mabel bake more cookies. The peace that Julie had found the night before in the snowdrift had lingered throughout the day. Although there were many moments when she thought of Livvy, wished she were here, there was also a calm acceptance of life without Livvy.

That evening, dinner was cold sandwiches. "Eat up," Mabel prompted. "People should start arriving within a half an hour."

"I can't eat," Chris said, shoving his plate aside.

"He always gets this way," Mabel told Julie. "It's like he gets sympathetic stage fright for all the kids."

"I just know how important this whole thing is for the kids and I want everything to be perfect," Chris answered.

Julie reached across the table and took his hand in hers, squeezing it reassuringly. "I'm sure everything will go just fine. The kids will be brilliant, and the audience will be awed." She withdrew her hand, suddenly self-conscious as she saw the warmth radiating from his eyes. It was a warmth that reminded her of how wonderful it had been to kiss him, how right it had felt to be held in his arms.

She picked up her sandwich, confused by the emotions that now raced through her. As the others continued to talk about the imminent program, the conversation whirled around her. She paid no attention, instead trying to sort out her strange feelings for Chris.

He'd been kind to her when she'd needed kindness. He'd offered her warmth to assuage the coldness of her grief. His kisses had overwhelmed her, his caresses had teased and tormented her. He'd breathed life back into her and forced her to accept her grief but get on with her life.

She would always be grateful to him for what he'd done for her, but did her feelings for him extend further? She was afraid to examine this too closely.

"I think I've got a long skirt and a red blouse upstairs that you're welcome to wear for the program tonight," Mabel said, bringing Julie from her confusing introspection. "They belonged to a girl who worked for us a couple months ago. She was about your size."

"I'd like that," Julie agreed, realizing she had nothing festive in her suitcase to wear for the special occasion. Besides, she felt festive and she knew Livvy would want her to embrace this night.

After supper, she changed into the clothes Mabel had given her, finding the blouse a perfect fit and the skirt waistband needing only a slight alteration with a safety pin.

Once dressed, she went back downstairs, entering the kitchen just as Chris hung up the phone receiver. "That was one of the women from the school. Jennifer Baker won't be able to be in the play. She's been quarantined with chicken pox."

"Oh, no. Did she have a big role?" Julie asked.

Chris shook his head. "She was the angel at the top of the ladder. We should be all right without her. She didn't have any lines or anything." He sat down at the table and raked a hand through his hair in distraction. "I just know how disappointed she'll be in missing all the fun. We'll have to figure out something special to do to make it up to her."

Julie nodded, touched that his first concern was for a little girl who wouldn't be able to be a part of the play. "Maybe we could take a little 'Merry Chicken Pox' party to her when she's feeling better," she offered, then blushed, remembering she wouldn't be here for much longer. "At least it's something you and Mabel and Doc could do for her," she added.

He nodded, jumping up as a horn sounded from outside. "That will be the kids," he said. "I'd better get out there. If they're left alone, they'll eat all the cookies before the guests ever arrive.''

"Would you like for me to come with you? I used to be pretty good at corralling kids.''

He smiled, putting an arm around her shoulders. "It would be terrific if you'd greet the people while I keep the kids occupied backstage.''

"I'll be glad to help Santa,'' she replied.

"Santa needs all the elves he can get, and you're the most attractive Christmas elf I've seen in years.''

As they walked across the snow toward the shed, Julie once again thought of how right it felt to be here, to have the warmth of Chris's arm around her.

It confused her, this feeling of rightness. She didn't quite know what to make of it. Nor was she sure she was ready to make anything of it. She'd only just made the decision to rejoin the living. It was much too soon to think of anything else.

"I'll talk to you later,'' he said, removing his arm from around her as they entered the shed.

She nodded, numbed by her strange emotions. She watched him as he rounded up the children and disappeared backstage. She slid into a seat, her mind still whirling. *Surely I can't be falling in love with Chris Kringle.* It just wasn't possible. Surely what she felt for him was gratefulness and friendship. And she felt a powerful physical pull for him, too. She had to admit it. But was that love?

Love was an emotion she thought she'd never welcome into her heart again, a feeling she'd been afraid had been buried with her daughter. It was too soon to even think she might be in love with anyone.

She jumped as she heard the sound of slamming car doors from outside. The guests had begun to arrive. She would have to think about Chris and her own crazy emotions later.

Within minutes, the shed was filled with people and the air of anticipation was thick. It was obvious to Julie that Chris was a man who was well liked in the area, and as his houseguest, she, too, was treated warmly by everyone.

Mabel and Doc stood by the refreshments and Julie grinned as she overheard them bickering over the proper way to serve punch. It seemed there was nothing the two agreed on, except for their affection for each other.

Minutes before the play was scheduled to begin, Chris hurried toward Julie, a video camera in his hand. "Would you mind taking a video of the play?" he asked.

"Not at all," she agreed, taking the camera from him.

"Thanks." He leaned over and gave her a quick kiss on the cheek, then hurried back to the stage area.

She reached up and touched her cheek, the imprint of his lips still burning her skin. He was a curious blend of goodness and sexiness, touching first her heart, then her hormones.

But I'm leaving here in a couple of days, she reminded herself. And she had no idea how Chris felt about her. Perhaps his kisses were nothing more than the way a warm, caring man expressed himself. She'd watched him with the kids, with Mabel and Doc, and she knew that hugs and kisses came easily from him.

He'd cared about her pain, recognized her as a person who hurt, but maybe his feelings for her didn't extend beyond that. The North Pole had been a wonderful place to begin to heal, but that didn't make it her home.

As music filled the shed, signaling the beginning of the play, Julie slid into a seat and concentrated on focusing the video camera. She didn't want to think about her feelings for Chris. Nor did she want to think about how she would feel when it was time to leave here. She simply wanted to enjoy this moment, with the sounds of Christmas swelling the air, and the efforts of the children who'd worked so hard to make this a special night. For this moment it was enough. It had to be.

The first half was wonderful. A play written by the children themselves, it was funny, at times nonsensical, but wonderful. The audience was appreciative, clapping often and filling the shed with their laughter. Julie kept the video camera whirring, capturing all the magic on film.

As the nativity scene began, Chris scooted into the seat next to her, his face lit with shining pride. "They're doing great, aren't they?"

She smiled and nodded at him. "Yes, they're terrific."

He gazed at her, a touch of worry pulling at his attractive features. "Are you all right?"

Her heart swelled, touched by his concern. "I'm fine," she answered. It was true. She'd been afraid that the children's laughter and their performance might be painful for her to watch.

There had been a brief moment in the first half of the program, when she'd thought of Livvy's face, remembered her bright smile as she'd sat on a department-store Santa's lap, whispering conspiratorially into his ear.

The memory had brought a touch of pain, a bittersweet moment of regret for all that would be no more, but it hadn't been the drowning grief she'd come to expect. Instead, the memory had warmed her heart, made her realize she was slowly healing, finding a comforting acceptance.

As the program drew to an end, the kids began singing "Silent Night." Julie sang along, finding a renewed faith, and a bittersweet joy in her heart. She focused the camera on each and every child, seeing the miracle of life on each of their faces.

She panned the camera to encompass the entire stage, freezing as she saw a little girl dressed like an angel atop the ladder.

Jennifer Baker was supposed to be the angel, and she had chicken pox. And Chris had said nobody else would play the part.

So who was the little angel?

Julie zoomed the lens in on the little girl, gasping and dropping the camera as she rose to her feet. It was Livvy. She was dressed all in white, a golden halo hovering crookedly above her head. Her smile bathed Julie in a warm, loving light.

Julie was vaguely aware of Chris's grasp on her arm, his voice filled with alarm as he called her name. But she didn't answer him, couldn't answer him. She was filled with the essence of Livvy and she was afraid that by moving a muscle, by making a sound, the image on top of the ladder would disappear.

Tears blurred her vision as she felt Livvy's spirit stir inside her. She could smell the sweet scent of her hair, feel her baby arms wrapped around her neck, hear her clear voice rising above the others. Julie shuddered, her soul flooded with her love for her daughter, and the sudden knowledge that Livvy was warm and happy, in a place filled with love.

A sob choked in her throat as Julie realized something else. Livvy was telling her goodbye, letting her know it was time to let go. Her crooked halo shone with a brilliance, and with a small wave, she disappeared.

Julie gasped, staring long and hard at the empty ladder.

"Julie ... for God's sake, are you all right?"

She became aware of Chris's worried concern and she turned to him, knowing her awe, her sense of wonder was in her eyes for him to see. "She was here," she said softly, the miracle still filling her heart. "Livvy was here." She smiled at Chris's perplexity, their conversation interrupted by the audience clapping and rising. The play was over. "I'll tell you about it later," Julie said, reaching out and taking his hand. "It's all right. I'm not crazy," she assured him, laughing at his bewilderment. "In fact, for the first time in a year, everything is really all right."

He looked at her dubiously and she merely laughed again.

Later that night, after the kids and the audience had gone home and Mabel and Doc had retired to their rooms, Chris sat on the sofa with Julie, listening intently as she told him of the vision of Livvy.

"I know it sounds crazy and impossible," Julie said. "But it was real. She was really there."

Chris didn't know if it had really happened or not. And what he believed or didn't believe didn't really matter, for he knew Julie believed she'd seen her daughter, and that was all that mattered. "Ah, the miracle of Christmas," he said, loving the new light that shone from her eyes, a light that banished the last traces of the darkness of her soul.

No matter what had happened, no matter what she'd seen atop that ladder, he knew Julie had finally said goodbye to her debilitating grief, and that in itself was a special kind of miracle.

He leaned back and placed an arm around her shoulders and together they stared at the fire he'd built earlier in the fireplace. He knew her thoughts were focused on Livvy and on her very own miracle, and his thoughts were completely fixated on her.

Earlier that morning Charley had delivered her car and it was now in the garage, ready to carry her away from the North Pole and back to Denver life. She wasn't aware that it was there, but Chris knew he'd have to tell her first thing in the morning.

It was time...time for her to return to her own life. He knew she would be all right. She was on her way to embracing life again. Yes, she was finally on her way, learning how to live without Livvy.

He sighed, breathing in the scent of her light perfume, the smell of her silken hair. He savored the warmth of her body so close to his, trying to ignore the responding heat that filled him.

Yes, she would be fine, and it was time to let her go. She would learn to live again, love again, without Livvy. Now all he had to worry about was how *he* would learn to live again, love again, without her.

Chapter Ten

Christmas morning. Julie opened her eyes and stretched languidly, at peace with herself for the first time in months. For a long moment she merely lay in bed, replaying the night before, the miracle of Livvy during the play and later, the contentment of sitting with Chris's arm around her, watching the flames dance in the fireplace.

I love him. The thought hit her with the unexpectedness of an icy snowball down the back. How had it happened? When had this man so utterly, so completely, stolen her heart?

She sat up, shoving her hair from her eyes, stunned by the sudden knowledge. *I'm in love with Chris*

Kringle. It flowed through her, like a sip of hot cocoa on a wintry night, warming her from the inside out.

She didn't know when it had happened. It might have been inside her for days. It was as if in releasing her grief, she'd opened her heart to acknowledge other emotions, and the one that winged through her, sure and strong, was love for Chris.

But how did he feel about her? He hadn't said or done anything that would lead her to believe he saw any future in their relationship. Sure, they had shared a couple of kisses, a few caresses—but those had been the unexpected result of his attempt to soothe her grief, and their mutual attraction. She was hardly so naive to think those kisses meant anything more.

She lay there, filled with the wonder of her love, but confused as to what to do about it. She had a life in Denver, and as much as she'd come to love the North Pole, it wasn't her home. She would be leaving here as soon as her car was ready.

Chris had a full life here. He had the children from the school, his work as Santa, the companionship of Doc and Mabel, the respect of the people of the area. He didn't need her, and she suddenly realized that she needed to be needed.

She got out of bed and stood beneath the hot spray of the shower, her heart filled with a different kind of pain as she thought of leaving the North Pole, leaving Chris.

Maybe it's just gratefulness, she told herself a few minutes later as she got dressed. Chris had done so much for her, helped her through so much, that she wondered if perhaps she was mistaking gratefulness for love.

Surely that's it, she told herself, somewhat relieved by this new assessment of her emotions. She would leave here and get on with her life, and she would always be grateful to Chris for all he had done for her.

With that straight in her mind, she headed downstairs and into the kitchen.

"Merry Christmas," Mabel greeted her cheerfully.

"Uh . . . Merry Christmas," Julie returned, trying not to stare at the oversize rhinestone earrings that dangled from Mabel's ears.

Mabel grinned at her knowingly. "I know, I know. They're horrible, aren't they?" She reached up and touched one of the shoulder-length earrings. "Aren't they the most gaudy things you've ever seen?" Her smile softened. "Doc gave them to me. Said he saw them in the store and was caught by their brilliance and sparkle." Mabel's cheeks flushed a pretty pink.

"He told me it would take a very special woman to wear them, and he thought I was pretty special."

On impulse, Julie hugged the old woman close. "Chris and Doc are lucky to have you," she said. She stepped back and smiled. "And I want to thank you for allowing me to be a part of your Christmas this year."

"I should be thanking you for your help with all the cookie baking and the cleaning," Mabel protested. "You've been a nice addition here," she said gruffly, then cleared her throat. "Why don't you grab that tray there with the coffee cups. We always have coffee by the tree on Christmas morning."

"There you are." Chris stood up as Julie entered the great room. He took the tray from her and set it on the coffee table. "Doc and I were wondering if you'd get up in time to join us in our customary Christmas morning coffee."

Julie smiled, suddenly unaccountably shy with him as she thought of the strange thoughts that had assailed her when she'd first awakened.

"Did you sleep well?" Doc asked.

"Wonderfully," Julie answered, sitting down on the sofa near Chris.

"Here we are," Mabel said as she entered the room carrying a coffeepot and a platter of cinnamon rolls. "This is my special Christmas morning blend of coffee," she explained to Julie as she poured them each a cup of the fragrant brew.

"Mmm," Julie murmured, taking a sip. "I taste cinnamon, but there's something else."

"Ah, Doc and I have been trying to figure it out for the past couple of years," Chris explained. "But we can't get her to tell us the secret ingredient."

"Christmas magic—that's the secret," Mabel exclaimed with a mysterious grin.

As the conversation turned to a rehashing of the play the night before, Julie found her gaze drawn again and again to Chris. It was as if she was seeing him for the first time, without the dulling blanket of sadness in her heart to veil his image.

He was clad in jeans and a bright red sweater that served to emphasize the strength and broadness of his shoulders, the dark, richness of his hair. She remembered the kisses they had shared, kisses that had stirred her down to her very toes. No, it wasn't just gratefulness she felt for him. It *was* more...much, much more.

"Julie?"

She realized Mabel had asked her something and now looked at her expectantly. "I'm sorry. What did you say?"

"I was just saying you'd better grab one of those cinnamon rolls before Chris eats them all."

"Oh, I'm really not hungry," she replied, smiling self-consciously at Chris. "Go ahead and help yourself to mine."

He grinned, looking wonderfully sexy, and reached for another of the sweet rolls. "If you bake these too often, Mabel, I won't have to pad my Santa costume."

"Well, while you're stuffing your face, I've got a present for Julie," Mabel said, reaching for a gaily wrapped package beneath the tree.

"Oh, you shouldn't have," Julie said, embarrassed that she hadn't even thought about gifts for these people who had given so much of themselves to her. She accepted the gift from Mabel and opened it, finding a hand-knitted scarf in beautiful blue hues. "Oh, Mabel, it's beautiful," she exclaimed, wrapping it around her neck.

"I've got a little something for you, too," Doc said, handing her another wrapped package. Julie opened it, laughing as she saw what it contained. A first-aid kit for the glove compartment of the car.

"I'll never travel without it," she said, rising off the sofa and delivering a kiss to Mabel, then planting one on Doc's cheek.

"Come back over here and sit down," Chris said, patting the sofa next to him. "I can't let the two of them show me up. I've got a present for you also."

Julie sat down next to him, trying to ignore the way his scent filled her senses, the way his nearness threatened to obliterate everything else from her mind. She took the tiny present he offered her, carefully removing the bright paper. Her breath caught in her throat and tears sprung to her eyes as she held up a delicate, wood-carved angel.

"Oh, Chris...!" she exclaimed, too touched to complete her thanks.

He smiled at her, his eyes warming her as he gazed at her. "With Livvy, you'll always have an angel on your shoulder, but I thought it might help if you had one you could keep in your pocket."

Tears clung to her lashes, then spilled over onto her cheeks as she stared at all three of them. "I... I don't know what to say."

"I do," Chris said. "You kissed Mabel and Doc.... Now where's mine?"

With an embarrassed laugh, she leaned forward, intent on kissing his cheek as she had done to the other two. But at the last minute, he turned his head so it was their lips that met. The kiss was quick, but lingered long enough for her to taste the cinnamon sweetness of his mouth and the deeper flavor of something else...some indefinable emotion that stole her breath away.

She broke the kiss with another embarrassed laugh, scooting away from him on the sofa.

"I have one other present for you," he said, holding up the keys to her car. "Charley delivered your car yesterday. It's in the garage, all ready to take you home."

"Oh...oh, that's wonderful," she said, forcing the words from her protesting lips. "Then I guess I can get on my way today." She waited for Chris to say something, anything that would let her stay, but he merely nodded, averting his gaze from her.

"You can at least wait until after lunch," Mabel said. "I've got a big turkey cooking in there and we're going to have it with all the trimmings."

"I don't think so," Julie said, rising from the sofa, knowing that putting off leaving would only make it that much more difficult. "If I leave now, I'll get back to Denver well before dark." She looked at them all, her gaze lingering on Chris, who sat staring at the Christmas tree. "If you all will excuse me, I'll just go get packed."

Home. It's time to go home, she thought minutes later as she folded her clothes and placed them back into her suitcase. But the thought of her apartment in Denver offered her no sense of homecoming.

But I've got a life in Denver, she told herself firmly, shutting the suitcase and snapping the latch.

A life that for the past year had been achingly empty and without meaning.

I can change that. I can make new friends, re-establish myself as a functioning, productive person. She had to go home. The North Pole wasn't her home. Yet, even as she told herself all these things, there was an empty ache in her heart as she thought about leaving here.

She dug for the inner strength Chris had told her she possessed within. She would survive this. She would survive the heartache of loving Chris and leaving him behind. But that didn't make the ache any less intense.

Picking up her suitcase, she walked slowly back down the stairs. She couldn't stay here unwanted, unneeded. It was obvious Chris was a caring, wonderful man, but he wasn't her man.

"Well, I guess this is goodbye," she said with a forced brightness as she stood in the doorway of the great room. She smiled at Doc and Mabel. "Thank you for all you've done. I'll never be able to repay you all."

"Just come and visit us whenever you can. You'll always be welcome here," Mabel said.

Julie nodded, although she knew she would never return. It would be too painful to come back for a visit.

"I'll walk you out," Chris said, taking her suitcase from her.

Together they walked out the back door and toward the garage. The sky overhead was gray, as gray as Julie's heart. How sad, that she had finally come to terms with one heartache only to make room for another. *It's not fair,* she railed inwardly, but as she looked up at Chris's stoic face, she realized life was never fair. She could only accept what was dealt to her and go on.

"It smells like snow," Chris observed as they reached the garage and he opened the door. "Hopefully you can make it back to Denver before it falls."

"I'm sure I'll be fine," she assured him, watching as he placed her suitcase in the trunk, then slammed it shut and handed her the keys.

For a long moment they merely looked at each other, his expression inscrutable, hers carefully schooled to hide the emotion that burst in her heart.

He reached up and touched the side of her face, his touch as soft as a snowflake against her skin. "Be well, Julie. Be happy," he said.

She swallowed hard against the lump that had grown in her throat. "I'll be fine, thanks to you. I don't know how to thank you for—"

"Don't." He withdrew his hand from her face. "The best thanks you can ever give me is to be happy."

She nodded, unable to speak, and he opened her car door. She hesitated before sliding in, drinking the vision of him in one last time. "Then . . . I guess this is goodbye," she whispered.

"Goodbye, Julie." His voice was as soft as a sigh.

She paused another minute, giving him every opportunity to stop her, to kiss her, to do anything to make her stay. Finally, realizing he wasn't going to do anything, she slid behind the wheel and pulled the door closed.

She remained strong as she started the engine, held back her tears as she backed out of the garage, stayed perfectly controlled as she put the car into Drive and headed out through the gates of the North Pole.

It wasn't until she looked in her rearview mirror and saw him standing in the snow amid the backdrop of the Christmas-wrapped house, that the tears began to glisten in her eyes. And it wasn't until he was completely out of her sight, that she pulled the car over to the side of the road and allowed the burning tears to fall.

Chris watched her car until it disappeared, trying to ignore the gnawing ache in the pit of his stomach...an ache that had nothing to do with hunger or illness.

She was gone, and he should feel wonderful. She was on her way back to where she belonged. The grief she'd arrived here with had finally ebbed to where it would not hamper her future happiness.

Yes, he should feel wonderful...so why didn't he? Why did he feel as if he'd just made the biggest mistake of his life in letting her go?

He heaved an enormous sigh and walked back to the house. Opening the back door, he saw Mabel standing in front of the oven, basting the turkey. She straightened up and looked at him. "So you just let her go?"

He shrugged and looked at her helplessly. "What else was I supposed to do?"

"Stop her, tell her you love her."

Chris flopped down in a chair at the table. "If she had wanted to stay, surely she would have. I think she was sent here for us to help her. We helped and now it's time to let her go."

Mabel stared at him in disgust. "So now you know for sure that you were supposed to just let her go without telling her that you love her? My, my, you must be on a direct line to the angels in heaven."

Chris grimaced. "You know that's not true. I don't know any more than anyone else."

"That's the truth," Mabel agreed with a nod. "So you can't know why Julie was brought here. You're always giving to everyone else.... Maybe Julie's love was meant to be a gift to you."

Chris stared at her, remembering the sweet sensuality of Julie's kisses, the sunshine beauty of her smile, the musical sound of her laughter. Had it been his job to help her heal, then let her leave and give those same things to another man? Had he cheated her by not telling her what was in his heart? Cheated himself?

He jumped up suddenly and headed for the door. "I'm going after her," he said.

"You better hurry," Mabel shouted after him as he ran to the stables.

It took him only minutes to hitch up the horses to the sleigh. He knew it would be more expedient to drive the car after her, but it somehow seemed right that he chase after her in the sleigh. Besides, he could cut across country in the sleigh.

He didn't care if he had to chase her all the way to Denver and park the horses outside her apartment building. He had to tell her he loved her. He didn't know if what she felt for him was mere gratefulness or something more, but he had to know.

The horses were frisky, as if sensing his urgency, and they took off at a brisk pace, running in the direction Chris knew she'd travel. The sleigh bells rang a merry tune, and in every tinkle, they seemed to sing her name.

Chris had no doubt that sooner or later he would catch up to her. What he didn't know was how she would react to him professing his love for her. As the sleigh slid through the snow, he asked for his own special Christmas miracle.

It was snowing. Julie saw the big fat flakes decorating her car window through the mist of her tears. She dried her cheeks with the back of her hand, realizing she needed to get on her way.

Before she could restart the car engine, she heard the distant sound of bells. Unsure she trusted her own ears, she rolled down her car window and listened. Sure enough, it was bells, and the sound was getting closer and closer.

She stepped out of the car, looking around curiously. Her breath caught in her throat as a set of horses, then a sleigh, suddenly crested the hill. The snow was coming down in earnest now, cutting visibility and making Julie wonder if perhaps the sleigh was merely a vision.

However, as it drew closer and she saw Chris, heard him calling her name, her heart began pounding in her chest. What was he doing? Why was he here?

He reined in the horses, stopping the sleigh next to her car. "Is something wrong with the car?" he asked, jumping down from the seat.

Julie shook her head. "No. What are you doing here?" she asked, afraid to hope, afraid to believe the expression in his blue eyes.

"I'm making a rescue," he said, standing directly in front of her.

"A rescue? But nothing is wrong with the car. I don't need to be rescued."

"No, but I do," he said softly, placing a hand on each of her shoulders.

"I . . . I don't understand," Julie answered in confusion, noting how the falling snow was sticking to his hair and beard, reminding her of the very first time she'd seen him.

He dropped his hands, shoving them instead into his jeans pocket. "I've developed this horrible sickness."

"What sort of sickness?" Julie asked breathlessly.

"Lovesickness." The blue of his eyes penetrated her, filling her with a sort of joyous wonder as he continued, "Julie, I know you've been going through a rough time and you might not be emotionally ready to hear what I have to say, but I can't live with myself if I don't tell you what's in my heart."

"Tell me." She held her breath in anticipation, afraid to hope, afraid to anticipate what he needed to say.

"I love you, Julie. I want to share my home with you. I want to share my life with you." He ran a hand through his snow-studded hair. "I know you might not be ready to love again. But I know Livvy..."

"Would want me to love again," Julie said, her heart filled to bursting. "Oh, Chris, the best tribute of my love for Livvy is to continue to laugh, continue to live, continue to love. And I want to do it here, at the North Pole, with you."

Before she could say anything more, she was in his embrace, his lips on hers, working their own special brand of magic.

As his lips slowly left hers, she laughed, a bubbling release of joy. "If I'm not mistaken, Mr. Claus wasn't a solo act. There was a Mrs. Claus who took care of his bookkeeping and made sure the electricity didn't get shut off."

"To heck with the bills," Chris said, the blue of his eyes intensifying. "I need you to share my dreams and my hopes. I want you beside me through the nights. I want to share your laughter and your tears. I want to share your memories and your future. Will you marry me, Julie?"

"Yes... oh, yes," she breathed, and as his lips claimed hers once again, she realized that the true miracle of Christmas was in the miracle of love.

"It's time now," the deep voice said to Livvy.

She nodded, content. Yes, it was time to go now. She knew her momma was going to be fine. Someday they would be together again, but in the meantime Livvy was satisfied knowing her mother would be happy.

She stood up and reached for the hand that awaited hers. The hand was warm, infinitely loving as it closed around her smaller one.

She started walking, but paused a moment, turning back and taking one last look. "Goodbye, Momma," she whispered, blowing a kiss. Then, turning back around, she walked toward the welcome warmth of the brilliant light. As she went, she reached up with one hand and carefully straightened her halo.

*   *   *   *   *

**HE'S MORE THAN
A MAN, HE'S
ONE OF OUR**

**REBEL DAD
Kristin Morgan**

When Linc Rider discovered he was a father, he was determined to find his son and take him back. But he found that Eric already had a home with his adoptive mother, Jillian Fontenot. The choice wouldn't be easy: take the boy from such a beautiful, loving woman or leave his son behind. And soon it was too late to tell Jillian the real reason he'd spent so many days in her home—and in her arms....

Join Linc in his search for family—and love—in Kristin Morgan's REBEL DAD. Available in January—only from Silhouette Romance!

Fall in love with our Fabulous Fathers!

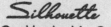

ROMANCE™

Take 4 bestselling love stories FREE

Plus get a FREE surprise gift!

UNDER THE MISTLETOE

*Where's the best place to find love
this holiday season?* UNDER THE MISTLETOE,
*of course! In this special collection, some of
your favorite authors celebrate the joy of the
season and the thrill of romance.*

Available in December from

Silhouette
ROMANCE™

SRXMAS

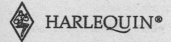

Christmas Classics

Share in the joys of finding happiness and exchanging the ultimate gift—love—in full-length classic holiday treasures by two bestselling authors

JOAN HOHL
EMILIE RICHARDS

Available in December at
your favorite retail outlet.

Only from  *Silhouette*® where passion lives.